Sins of the Fathers

Sins of the Fathers

S. Gepp

A
Grinning Skull Press
Publication
PO Box 67, Bridgewater, MA 02324

DEDICATION

For David & Larissa.

And for Clare S. from so long ago.

CONTENTS

Acknowledgments

I would like to thank Grinning Skull Press for taking a chance on this obscure author and giving *Sins of the Fathers* a home.

Chapter One

1991

Smoke covered the ground, forming a swirling fog. The flickering fires in two large braziers gave the only light to the scene; the dull new moon was hidden by the thick clouds that also obscured the stars. A bird's sudden call silenced the few insects, plunging the area into a desolate silence broken only by the crackling of the flames as they consumed their meager fuel.

Gradually, other noises arose: the steady thud of slow footsteps pacing across moist earth, the rustle of heavy objects pushing past trees and shrubs, labored breathing. And with all that came a final, softer sound, one that was irregular and muffled, almost drowned out by the footfalls. Methodical, constant, and incessant, the slow march of weary soldiers, growing progressively louder.

At one end of the vacant clearing, the bushes rustled and shifted, and seven hooded figures trudged carefully forward, a long, wriggling plastic bag borne between them all. The one in the lead lit their way with a burning brand that was placed carefully in the first brazier they passed, releasing an explosion of sparks, living creatures fleeing the fires, rising desperately into the air before petering out.

The seven barely noticed as they made their way to the center of the small glade, the high trees that surrounded them giving it the feel of a natural fortress, of protection, of sanctuary.

They stopped and waited briefly. The one at the rear, whose hands cradled something inside the bag, nodded once, and they all carefully placed their burden on the ground. The movements within grew more frantic even while the other noises that tried to emerge remained distorted and blanketed. But the seven figures merely stepped back and watched.

An owl hooted, another responded in kind. One of the people cast a nervous glance around from beneath the cowl, but that was the only acknowledgment of the outside world. This same person then shrank down, the stance one of submission, lacking the confidence of the rest.

The one who had been at the rear moved a little, and the others followed suit so that they formed a loose circle around their package, the nervous one the last to move.

A pair of eyes, glowing yellow in the contained light, peered out from the underbrush, wary of the strange smells. The bag gave a sudden, violent spasm and the forest creature bolted, making a few nocturnal birds rise into the dark sky and disappear into the night.

Six of the figures did not flinch. They merely waited. Their time was not yet at hand.

Yet the head of the other bowed even lower and shook from side to side.

The action was ignored by the rest.

2012

"A funeral? Anyone I know?"

"That's hardly the question to ask." Troy Washington looked at his son and shook his head, scowling. "But, for your information, no, it's not anyone you know. It's for an old friend." He paused as he adjusted his tie in the mirror. "I haven't seen him for, hell, twenty-odd years, I reckon." He gave up on the tie. "His kid died."

"So, why are you going to his funeral?"

Troy faced the sixteen-year-old standing in the door of his bedroom. "It's hard to explain," he said lamely before offering a wan half-smile, the insincerity evident. "Look, Sam, I know I'm going to miss the game this afternoon..."

"It's the first final," his son grumbled with the faux dejection of someone who knew his words were futile but felt he had to make a token effort.

"And I appreciate that," Troy went on, "but remember, this is the first game I've missed all season."

"Sure, yeah." Sam shook his head. "Turning up for the last five minutes and playing with your phone is not the same as being there." He turned and stomped away, not bothering to wait for a response.

Troy merely stared at the mirror again, smoothed down his hair, then stepped back. He looked good enough for a funeral, he supposed as he ran his fingers over his wispy mustache. Now to go and make an appearance.

"So, seriously, who is this person?" He jumped a little and smiled half-heartedly as his wife, Ellen, joined him, making a final perfunctory adjustment to his tie and lapels, done on auto-pilot, the expression on her face bland.

"You were listening?" he asked with unconcealed irritation.

"Well, you've been in a foul mood ever since you got that thing in the post," Ellen shot back. Then she added, "Well, fouler than usual."

"Yeah, screw you," he grumbled, pushing past her to the bedroom door. "Now, I've got to get going."

She snorted at him. "Not going to tell me?" she muttered, her tone of voice bored. "Typical."

"Fine. It's not anyone you ever knew." He chewed his inner cheek. "It's not even someone I knew. His name was Simon O'Dowd."

"That car-crash kid? The one on the news?" Her expression showed incredulity. "Why in the hell would you get asked to that? I saw on TV last night it's being kept low-key and..."

"His old man was one of my best friends in high school. Happy?"

"And that's it? Why are you even going?"

Troy didn't respond as he made his way to the

other end of the house. Hell, she was right; why was he going?

He knew. It was all because of…

No, he didn't want to think about it. Everything they had done, and all for nothing. And now he was going to the funeral of Sean's son. It hardly seemed worth it. Nothing hardly seemed worth it.

All for absolutely nothing.

1990

Five young men sat in a circle, each reading a separate book, their school uniforms in various states of distress. A few derogatory words were cast in their direction by other members of their school community, but lifetimes of such abuse rendered them virtually impervious to any verbal slings and arrows.

One of the priests who served as a physics and general science teacher walked past and gave them a friendly wave. Two of the readers responded in kind. Teachers tended to like them; their high grades and general classroom demeanor was exactly what the school wanted— even expected—from its students, at least from its students who did not excel at sports. And except for Julian, and to a lesser degree Francis, that was them—the very antithesis of sportsmen.

It was Julian who approached them all now and sat down in their midst. "And how goes the Round Table?" he asked. They all smirked a little at the name, one they had given themselves four years earlier when they had first come together, purely by chance.

"Hey, ain't you lot missing a dwarf?" laughed one of a pair of larger students, prominent members of the football team, as they walked past.

"And aren't you missing a brain?" Julian returned.

The other's face clouded over immediately, and he started forward. "What did you say?" he demanded. The six of them merely stared at him with complete disdain. This was not an uncommon occurrence, but one they knew from past experience would go no further than words.

"You heard," Julian stated, closing his eyes and lying back on the grass, "or are you deaf as well as stupid?"

The student continued to stride forward, eschewing all previous behaviors they had come to expect. He reached down and grabbed Julian by the tie, yanking him to his feet. "What did you say?" he repeated.

"That you've just screwed up your final year."

The larger student dropped and spun quickly, fists balled up tight enough for his nails to draw blood from his palms. Francis stood there, his uniform immaculate, a copy of *The Hitchhiker's Guide to the Galaxy* in his hands.

The football player now rounded on this new arrival. "What, just because you're the chief school nerd, you think you can...what? What do you think?"

Francis smiled. "Your word against mine?" He laughed once. "You won't be sitting final exams; you'll get kicked off the football team, you'll..."

"You threatening me?" The larger student was growing increasingly more furious.

Then Sean stood and stumbled forward, teetered

briefly, then fell to his knees. Blood flowed down his face, but he was smiling. Then, in a blink of an eye, he fell and cried out. Luke rushed to his side before casting an accusing eye at the larger student.

"What… what…" the abusive football player blurted out, fear now suddenly taking hold of his emotions.

"Pretty sure we saw you do that," Brandon said.

Francis nodded. "And who are they going to believe? You? Or us?" he said quietly and calmly. "Say goodbye to going to university. That football career? Yeah, right. And do you really think Michelle Devereaux's family is going to let her keep seeing you after this?"

"You wouldn't." All color drained from his face. "You couldn't."

Brandon stood. "Maybe we don't have to," he stated. "Tell you what… If anyone says anything to us, does even the most pathetic practical joke, we'll blame you." The others held façades of solemnity on their visages, and, as one, they nodded their agreement.

"Like… like what?" the chastened boy mumbled, his eyes falling once again to Sean's bleeding forehead.

Troy pointed a little way off, to another larger youth watching with cautious curiosity. "He was an arsehole to us five minutes ago," he said. "Deal with him."

"Now," Francis barked.

Sean groaned louder and rubbed his forehead, spreading the blood around to emphasize the point. A long trickle ran down the side of his face. It was a trick he'd adapted from professional wrestling, but only these seven friends knew that from how often he'd done it to his older brothers; slicing through a dozen pimples and the upper layer of skin with a stone created a good blood flow.

Their antagonist said nothing more to them but walked away to confront the other boy, a fellow footballer. A subtle punch to the stomach doubled him over. No eyes fell back at the seven members of the self-proclaimed Round Table. But they all knew.

This was a perception of power—genuine power and influence; it was the first time they had ever felt anything like this in their lives. And for it to come now, at the beginning of their final year. The timing was perfect.

It felt good.

And they wanted more.

Chapter Two

2012

Troy sat at the back of his house, the chair nestled on the mud patch that had been waiting three years to become a deck or a porch or a verandah or anything, his seventh beer for the night in his hands, the other cans scattered on the ground around him. His head was buzzing, but in that unpleasant way he knew all too often led to nausea. Still, it was the only way he had been able to cope with the day.

In fact, just lately, it seemed to be the only way he could cope with anything.

No. Thinking like that was the path to... to what? Alcoholism? The dreaded "A" word his sister had used the last time he had spoken to her, maybe fourteen months earlier. No, he wasn't even close to being that far gone.

He threw the empty onto a pile of lawn clippings he'd promised to get rid of last weekend. Or maybe the weekend before. It didn't matter. Sam should do it anyway. He cracked the next can and settled back in the chair, trying not to think about the fact he'd been at the funeral of a seventeen-year-old boy, sitting with five of his six best friends from high school, close friends, friends until...

Her face flashed before his mind's eye.

"No," he whispered, trying to stop the unbidden tears from flowing too heavily.

Of course, seeing them again—especially at a funeral, especially at this time of the year—was going to bring her to mind. It made sense. It didn't make it any easier, but it did make sense.

He downed the rest of the beer without removing his lips from the metal container, the light-headedness washing over him immediately as the churning in his stomach rose uneasily to his throat. That can joined the last; number nine was taken up without hesitation.

A movement made him jump, but his bleary eyes were too slow in response. Probably a cat, that was all. Damn neighborhood seemed to be overrun with them lately. Just another cat, white and large and on his property. A large, white cat.

Very large.

He continued to gaze in that direction, chewing his inner cheek nervously. Whiteness... with more than a hint of gold?

Once more that face filled his memory. It was, until today, the face that only came to him in the depths of nightmares, one that had often proved impervious to the anaesthetizing effects of alcohol.

The funeral had been a bad one, and seeing those others, the Round Table, together again...

"Dad? You still out there?"

His son's voice sounded so far away. He looked at the second door, the one leading to the back room, the room they had given to Sam to give him a little more independence, leaving his old bedroom just right for when Troy felt the need to be away from Ellen for a night. Or a month. Or half a year and counting.

Troy stood uneasily on legs that no longer felt a part of his body and turned the handle.

It was unlocked.

That wasn't right. Sam never left his door unlocked, not since...

Hell, another memory Troy didn't need. Another time he was not proud of, and yet...

Troy opened it and strode boldly in, not giving these thoughts of the past any further purchase on his currently fragile grasp of reality.

He switched the light on without thinking. He was blinded. White dots flashed and flickered in front of his face. He stumbled about stupidly. A hand grabbed his shoulder. Life became a blur of movement, of color, of emotions he could not contain, of a brain not in control.

A face.

White and gold.

A blind panic; a manic flurry.

Reality returned.

So much blood. So, so much blood. Still gushing

from too many wounds. Still fresh and wet. Still…every-where.

He lifted the thin knife from the floor with hands that shook so much his sore, tired eyes could not focus on it. His head swam, and he could not really compre-hend what he was seeing, the scarlet fluid, the stillness, the mess…

Samuel Washington in the midst of it all.

He dropped the weapon and crawled across the pu-trid swamp and cradled his son's head in his arms. "Sam-my," he whispered. "Please, Sammy…"

"D-Dad?" That voice, so weak, so pathetic. "Dad, she was beautiful." He coughed, a bubble bursting on his lips, releasing its crimson contents. "Why, Dad?"

Sam's eyes closed one last time.

Troy could not even bring himself to cry. He simply held his son as close as he could, trying to remember the young man's childhood but unable to recall anything. Not anything at all.

And that was how Ellen found him an hour later.

And then the screaming began.

1991

One of the hooded figures looked at a watch, then dropped his arm to his side. Another brushed something off a hidden cheek.

A sudden pop in the brazier that now held the burn-ing brand made them all jump and glance at it uneasily. But none could look at the others, and each thanked the Powers That Be that their faces were hidden; each thought he was the only one who was scared and worried and downright terrified.

But they knew. They knew this would work. They told themselves they knew, and they told themselves they believed.

They told themselves this would make their lives perfect…

Six of them as firm in their convictions as they could be…

And one allowed the tears to flow down his shadow-enveloped cheeks. He had to stop this.

Chapter Three

2012

Francis Coulter stoically went through the indignity of a pat-down before allowing himself to be led into the small room, where he was seated at a table opposite Troy Washington. He'd seen this many times, but he'd never expected to be faced with one of his old friends on the other side, manacled at wrists and ankles, attached to a chair bolted to the floor, dressed in the drab colors of a prison uniform.

"You're my lawyer?" Troy whispered, his voice hoarse and dry.

"When I heard about it, I rang your wife—Ellen, isn't it?—and volunteered to work *pro bono* for you," he stated as he pulled a manila folder out of his crisp, clean briefcase, then a yellow pad, and finally a plastic sleeve. "It's odd," he said disinterestedly. "We don't have contact for twenty years and now twice in two days. Father Leckie would have said the hand of God was involved."

"The hand of something," Troy returned. "Yeah, something…"

Francis made a note on his pad and contemplated it. This was not the same man he'd gone to high school with. This man was defeated and had been for a long time. It was in his eyes and drawn face, in the sagging flesh of his cheeks, in the red eyes. None of this was new, and if he could see it, then a jury would also surely see it and judge him against it.

"Why did you do it?" Francis asked suddenly.

Troy stared back at him blankly before slowly but firmly shaking his head. "I didn't," was all he said, his voice so incredibly quiet.

Their eyes met. A truth was shared, a truth that made Troy out to be a liar right here, right now.

Francis sighed and opened the folder. He shoved the top photograph across the table and watched as Troy flinched away from the image, recoiling as though he had been shot but unable to take his eyes off the scene of blood-soaked death it depicted. He stretched a shaking hand towards it, but the chains prevented him from reaching it. Instead, he closed his eyes and turned his head, shaking it as the tears built up under his eyelids.

"What happened?" Francis asked without emotion.

"I don't know," Troy managed.

"Hell, mate," Francis groaned in exasperation. "It does not look good. Your prints and your son's were the only ones on the murder weapon, you were covered with his blood, you had a blood alcohol reading of point three. Point three! Six times the legal driving limit! Christ, Troy, how much had you had to drink?"

"A few cans last night, some wines after the funeral, a couple of Scotches when I got home."

"Nine cans of beer, seven glasses of wine, two full bottles of Scotch, plus the rest Ellen didn't know about," Francis stated coldly.

"A bit, then, I guess," he murmured finally, his words edged with depression.

"And then there's this." Francis slid the plastic sleeve across the table. Troy gazed at it and winced. It was the police report from thirteen months earlier. Drunk again, he had gone to the back room, forgetting in his haze that it had recently been given to Sam as his bedroom, and so he had thrown Sam out of the bed, splitting open the boy's forehead, the wound requiring eleven stitches to close.

Troy could not say anything.

Francis leaned back on his chair. "Look, mate, I don't want to bring you down, but you're fucked," he stated simply. "Seven puncture wounds to the heart. Man, this is bad."

Troy just stared back at him, the tears finally breaking free and flowing down his face without restraint. "I di...didn't...didn't do...do it," he hiccoughed pathetically.

Francis dropped his voice low. "We both know you're capable of..."

"It wasn't me!" he screeched.

"Tell me everything that happened then. Do not

leave a single thing out." Francis moved his body forward again, pen poised. "*Everything*," he emphasized.

Troy closed his eyes and dragged Francis back to a time so recent, yet one he really wanted to forget but knew he never could.

1990

Lord Acton said that power corrupts. Unfortunately for most, this realization does not come until it is too late.

Francis grabbed Brandon by the arm and dragged him into the boys' bathroom. Before his friend could say anything, he clamped a hand over his mouth and dragged him to the far wall. "Have a look," he whispered, pointing at the window.

Brandon smiled. The other side of the wall was the hastily constructed and poorly designed girls' bathroom, built when the school started to admit female students in the final two years of secondary schooling, just over a decade earlier, and thanks to a poorly placed mirror array, any girls not in a stall—normally those getting changed for whatever reason—were fair game to their male peers who knew about this anomaly.

Brandon carefully climbed onto the rim of the garbage bin, balanced there for a few moments, then lifted himself, hoping beyond all hope it would be the stunningly beautiful Chelsea Hartog changing into—or better yet, out of—her tennis uniform. Instead, what he saw very nearly made him fall off his makeshift pedestal.

He was visibly shaking when Francis finally managed

to get him outside.

"That was… That was…"

"Yeah, it was," Francis smiled. "I don't know the boy he was with…"

"I do. He's a couple of years younger than us." Brandon's face finally creased into a slight smile. "That's not good," he mused, the grin widening with each word.

"Our school captain in a…well…a clinch with a younger boy?" Francis pondered this briefly. "Not good for him, maybe. But us? Oh yeah, it's very good." He laughed out loud. "Come on, we need to tell the others."

"And then we'll have a discussion with a younger student about his future at the school," Brandon added with a self-satisfied nod.

Knowledge is indeed power, and these two had just had another tiny taste of the power they felt they had been denied for so long and now craved. Desperately.

Chapter Four

2012

Francis's hand shook a little as he downed his neat bourbon in one gulp. Too many bad memories had surfaced in the past week, painful memories of a youth that should have been perfect, and so soon after the anniversary. A stupid, youthful indiscretion…

Hang on. Youthful indiscretion? Was that how he was justifying the horrific action they had performed? It was terrible, and the fact they had all simply got on with their lives afterward was something for which they would never be forgiven, at least by themselves. He had gone back—as he did every year—less than two weeks earlier, and now it was all being hurled back in his face like a vicious slap.

He held up a finger, and the middle-aged man behind the bar nodded. "Make it three," said a voice from Francis's left. He looked sideways curiously and felt the smile break across his face before the emotion registered.

Julian and Luke sat down beside him, two men he had been estranged from for two decades, but who he was very glad to see now…even if they were part of that terrible memory that was always there, digging at him with guilt-tinged fingers. "Hey, guys," he said, his voice cracking more than he would have expected. "Good to see you here."

"Yeah, you, too, mate," Julian smiled, offering his hand. The shake was firm and enthusiastic, the years falling away far more easily than they had at the funeral a few days earlier.

"Look, no offense, but you look like shit," Luke stated as he also took the lawyer's offered hand.

"Yeah, I know." The barman placed the drinks in front of them all and took the money from Julian. "But look…thanks for coming, guys." He looked past them. "Any idea where the others are?"

"Brandon's on his way. He offered to get hold of Randy, uh, Randolph. I don't know about Troy." Julian looked down at his drink and grimaced. "I didn't feel right calling Sean. The wife and I are catching up with him and his missus tomorrow night, just for a catch-up, introduction, whatever, but Simon's death has really hit him hard."

"Sean? Yeah, I saw him this arvo." Brandon's voice made them jump as he dragged a chair over to them. "He's going real bad. Sorry. Oh, and hi," he finished with an embarrassed grin.

"Hey, everyone. What's up?" Randolph entered, the only one of the five not dressed in a shirt and tie. He leaned against the bar and stared at everyone else. "Fuck, what's up with you lot?" he stated.

"It's Sean. What do you think we..." Brandon started.

Francis was shaking his head, then stood. "Let's move," he muttered. "Somewhere less public."

"Hang on, what about Troy? I know he's always late, but shouldn't we at least wait?" Julian asked curiously. Luke nodded his agreement.

"Not an issue," Francis mumbled.

"Come on," Luke sighed, shaking his head.

Francis grimaced, then nodded at the barman, who returned the gesture. Without saying a word, Francis led them to a room off to one side where a low table was surrounded by comfortable chairs, which they took up slowly and with some confusion. Moments later, a young waitress appeared with a tray of finger food and two pitchers of beer, a second one following behind with plates and glasses. Francis offered them a smile as they left, closing the door behind them.

"This is all very serious," Randolph smiled as he took a small pie. "Someone else died?"

"Yes."

Randolph stopped in mid-bite while Brandon's arm jerked, spilling beer across the table.

"What?" Luke hissed.

Francis let out a long sigh but said nothing. Julian grunted and pulled a packet of cigarettes from his pocket. They all watched as he tapped one out and lit it, then inhaled deeply. The smoke curled up to the extraction fan and disappeared, everyone staring in mute fascination, glad to be distracted, even momentarily.

When Francis continued, it was reluctantly. 'Troy's been arrested. He's in the Remand Center in town. It'll be in tomorrow's papers, I'm sure. It somehow didn't make the TV news tonight, but I reckon by now it'll be all over the Net."

There was a long pause. "Shit, what'd he do?" Luke eventually croaked.

Francis watched Julian take a draw on his cigarette, breathing out the plume through his nose this time. "It appears he got drunk and..." Francis swallowed hard, his mouth drying up quickly, his tongue cleaving to the roof of his mouth uncomfortably. "The police say he killed his son," he finally finished.

Stunned silence greeted the statement. Julian's cigarette hung limp. Drinks remained untouched. Eyes were dropped or averted. "What... What happened?" Luke finally asked.

"He stabbed the kid. In the chest. Seven times."

The others finally exchanged glances. "But... But why?" Brandon managed.

Francis shook his head and shrugged. "He claims he didn't even do it." Brandon slid a beer in front of him. "I'm representing him, and I've known him for years, and even I don't believe him."

"Yeah, but, we know why..." Randolph muttered quietly.

"Before the funeral the other day, I hadn't seen him since he dropped out of uni," Luke said quickly. "I hardly recognized him."

"I kept in touch for a little while," Julian said. "But, you know, shit happens."

"Why did he just drop out of everything?" Brandon piped up. "I never understood that."

"*We* dropped out. Remember?" Randolph stated blandly.

"But you got an apprenticeship, then a good job," Francis said. "Troy just got stuck at a shipping company doing inventory on a computer."

"And drinking," Julian added. "Like I said, I kept in touch for a few years, but he drank so much, even back then. Even after Sam was born..." His voice trailed off as he realized what he'd been talking about. "Sam. Little Sammy," he muttered. "For fuck's sake, I was at his christening."

"He had his kids christened?" Randolph asked. "Even after..."

They were all aware just what he was referring to, and they were all glad he stopped himself. That had been the real reason why Troy and Randolph had dropped out of university, no matter what other excuses they may have convinced themselves of. It had been why Luke had changed his course to a teaching degree, why Brandon had taken a gap year in the middle of his journalism studies, and why Sean had transferred to a different university to finish his accounting degree. Only Francis's law aspirations and Julian's physics studies—which had eventually led to a Ph.D.—seemed to have been unaffected, but it was obvious that that was how those two had coped: by dedicating themselves whole-heartedly to their studies, blocking out the real world they had so appallingly affronted.

Francis broke the ensuing silence, and that memory they were all trying so hard to shove back into the dark recesses of their minds was brought starkly to the fore. "That's just it," Francis murmured. "He said he had a vision of…of her right before he found Sam. And then he held Sam as he died. It took twenty-one years, but what he did, what he started, it finally got all too much for him."

No-one could respond. The past would not let them speak. It had them in its thrall, and it was not about to let go, especially now that it had forced itself back into their lives.

1991

One of the figures reached under the drab-colored robe it wore and pulled out a knife, long and thin, the clean, sharp blade catching the glow of the flickering flames, giving it an orange sheen, the appearance of internal heat, a weapon forged of the very elements themselves.

A second followed suit, then a third, a fourth, two at the same time.

The final paused before slowly, with apparent reluctance, falling into line, with head still bowed.

Seven knives.

"We can't do this."

A whispered voice, floating on the air, coming from

seemingly out of nowhere.

"It's too late now." A returning voice, hoarse with emotion.

"No, it's not." The first voice was a little more confident.

"This is for us, remember. For what we desire most in the world." A third voice, the dominant sense coming through the words one of anger.

"How can it work?" Still, that terrified but dissenting first voice wanted to resist.

"Because it has worked already." A different, slightly higher pitched voice. All heads turned in the direction of the one who had been at the rear. There was no real answer to that, not one they felt they could make.

There was no answer to what was seen as the truth.

Chapter Five

2012

"You okay, dad?"

Francis poked his head into the front room of his house and looked at his son, hunched over the computer, books scattered and open on a folding table he had set up beside his chair. The eyes that stared at Francis from under a floppy fringe of black hair were a mirror of his own, something he had never really grown used to. "Sure. Why?" he asked with a forced smile.

The young man leaned back in his chair in a pose Francis's secretary would have recognized immediately. "Well, you're out late on a work night, you fumbled with your keys coming into the front door, and your clothes are a bit of a mess." His mouth curved into a mischievous grin. "And would I be able to smell alcohol on your breath if I came close enough?"

Francis held his hands up. "Guilty as charged, your honor," he said, and they both tittered at an old, old shared joke. "Regular Sherlock Holmes, aren't we? Sure you won't try to get into law next year instead of psychology?" Francis smirked.

"Nice try at changing the subject," the youngster stated. "There's only so many ways I'm following in your footsteps, and law's not one of them."

"But I was never school captain," Francis corrected. "And was definitely never on the football team."

"And I won't be Dux of the school, but that's by the by, and you know it." He folded his arms across his broad chest. "So, what's wrong, dad?"

Francis sighed and leaned against the door frame. Since he and Kellianne had divorced, his relationship with his son had slowly changed from the standard parent–child form he had 'enjoyed' with his own father to one more akin to friendship, so much so that at age fifteen the young man had opted to shift from his mother's home to his father's, leaving his younger brother and sister behind. Francis had subsequently gained the distinct impression that his daughter had been discouraged from following suit by her eldest brother, but he would never say anything. There was no way he wanted to lose what they had over something he could not be sure of.

"Dad?"

"Sorry, Nathan," he muttered. "Lost in my thoughts."

"Yeah, something's wrong. Spill." His words might have been a little flippant, but the tone of his voice and facial expression were scarily adult.

"I think I've got another funeral," he mumbled. "The son of another friend."

"Two?" There was more concern in his son's voice than Francis had been prepared for.

"Afraid so." Francis pushed himself away from the wall. "It's not good, either."

"Another old high school friend? Those guys you haven't seen in, like, twenty years?" Nathan leaned forward. "Dad, is something going on?"

"Coincidence," Francis said quickly. He was about to explain himself when the opening bars of AC/DC's "Thunderstruck" came from his pocket. He pulled his phone out and could not hide his surprise at the name on the screen.

"Who is it?" Nathan asked.

"Sandra." Francis continued to stare at the screen. "What's she calling me at this hour for?"

"Probably a client in trouble," his son suggested as the music sounded again. The young man knew the efficient and officious Sandra all too well; her hiring had been the straw that had broken the back of his parents' marriage. He still found himself wondering if it would have come to a head like it had if his mum had known Sandra's actual sexual preference. But his mum had seemed to have been searching for "the other woman" for as long as Nathan could remember, and so he supposed that Sandra had just been convenient.

Francis finally took the call. "Hey, Sandra, what's..." All color drained from Francis's face. "Th-thanks," he managed. "No, no, tell her I'll go down." He winced. "Now, yeah, right away, right. Thanks, Sandra. And... yeah. Thanks." He disconnected and stared at it as if it had suddenly bitten him.

"Dad, you look like you're about to throw up." Nathan was at his side before he had even noticed that the young man was moving.

Francis looked at him and shook his head slowly. "No, I don't think I will," he muttered. "But... It's my friend Troy, the one who... Shit. He's...he's... Shit, Nathan, he's dead."

1990

Troy sniffed at the air and wrinkled his nose. The atmosphere felt dry, and the odor of mildew hung like an invisible cloud over everything. He shuddered a little and glared at Julian. "Tell me again what we're doing in here," he whispered curtly.

"We're looking for a book," Julian replied in the same hushed tone.

Troy looked around at the rows and rows of shelving. "Well, duh," he shot back.

The old man seated behind an antique desk glared at them. They both shrank back a little, then giggled like the schoolboys they were and hustled away from him. "Okay, so what's the book?" Troy asked. "You've been way mysterious about this."

Julian's smile had not faded. "You know how we've been sort of doing the whole knowledge-is-power thing," he whispered, and yet he still cowered as his voice echoed through the empty corridors created by the tomes lined up all around them. "Well, I heard there's a book here that'll suit what we're after—knowledge we should not have."

"So, why do you need me?"

Julian stretched his arms out. "This is a big place," he said. "Two are better than one. And, before you ask, if we got any of the other guys down here as well, then, well, shit, with our carrying on, there's a chance we'd be banned for life."

"You're kidding," Troy smiled. Julian merely shook his head, and Troy looked nervously around. "Okay, so now I can ask… What the hell is this place?"

"Book repository," Julian explained. "The sorts of books that are never actually borrowed but are still thought to be of use. This is basement level one, and down the stairs is, obviously, level two. But if we want to go all the way down to basement level three, we'd need to get written permission from the Dean of our faculty."

Troy's smile was condescending. "Jules, we're not at uni yet," he reminded his friend.

Julian hushed him quickly, then pulled out a student ID card that indicated he was enrolled in undergraduate science. Troy struggled to stifle a gasp and decided that now—and especially here—was not the time to ask where he'd managed to get it.

"So, what are we looking for then?" Troy asked finally, gazing over the spines of the volumes, the leather-bound, the faded, the ripped and torn, the old and decrepit.

"A textbook. Matriculation chemistry, pre-World War Two, say nineteen thirty-two, thirty-three. It's called *Chemical Processes* or *Chemistry Processes*," he explained.

"So why are we looking for that?" He was confused; what could be in an old chem textbook that wasn't in their current one? Surely the standards of education hadn't dropped that markedly in fifty years.

"There's some awesome pracs in there. Making grain alcohol, making base anesthetics, and—" His grin suddenly returned. "—making nitroglycerine and base LSD."

"What?!" He quickly covered his mouth.

"Look, back then, only the rich and super-intelligent did matric, especially something like matric chem. They were the elite of society, and people thought they could be trusted with that sort of info."

"Hang on. How do you know this isn't some sort of urban myth or something?" Troy was immediately suspicious.

"Grandpa told me about it a couple of weeks ago. He asked me about my chem lessons, and he told me what they did back then." Julian's enthusiasm was quickly overwhelming Troy. And if Dr. Victor Worthington, one of the most highly regarded old scholars of their school, said something, then it was undoubtedly true.

"Okay. So, now what?" Troy looked about eagerly.

"You check in teaching resources, I'll go to the science section."

"And you're sure it's here?"

"If it's not here, then it's not going to be found by us." And with that less-than-hearty endorsement, they separated.

Thus it was that Troy, searching down in a corner of basement level two, found the book. Not the one they had come to find, but a book that intrigued him nevertheless. It was clearly out of place, stowed in a recess behind a series of grammar textbooks dating back to the first decade of the twentieth century. The pages were yellow, some spotted with green, and at some point in its life, a bookworm had drilled through the top corner. *A Treatise, Examination, and Relation of Nefarious Rituals in the Moor Country* by one Dr. Rev. B.L. Barnes; the front splash page gave its publication date as 1877, this edition from two years later. He could not believe it. He was holding a book one hundred and eleven years old. He flicked through it, and the smile that crossed his lips was not one of elation, and yet it was scarily genuine.

Chapter Six

2012

To Francis, that night felt like a bad dream that he was being forced to walk through, one that he couldn't wake from no matter how hard he tried.

The body was still on the floor of the holding cell. At least they'd cut him down, Francis decided, but that was the only small mercy to be thankful for.

The officers on duty barely acknowledged his credentials as they allowed him into the corridor so he could peer through the trap in the cell door.

The eyes were open, bulging out and staring up at nothing, but imploring all the same. The swollen, purple face looked barely human, its tongue filling the mouth, trails of mucus streaming out from the nose. His jumper was still wrapped around his neck, hiding any marks. Frances tried to look up, but the angle was awkward, so he couldn't tell where the deed had been done. Not that it mattered.

He couldn't help but gaze again at the corpse, with its permanent expression of confusion and begging. He cocked his head to one side. The left eye was blood-shot and the cheek beneath it definitely larger and more discolored than the rest of the face. A smudge of blood sat in the corner of the mouth; just a smudge, but now that the initial shock was wearing off, to Francis it stood out starkly. He cast a quick glance at the officer beside him, then back at his old high school friend.

"All right, counselor, I think that's enough." The officer's tone was firm and not a little threatening. Francis had no doubts that Troy had taken his own life. But he also had no doubt that Troy's circumstances had deteriorated substantially in here after Francis had left him. A suicide by name; so, what was it by any other term?

"Thank you," he responded blandly and hurried away from the scene. He could not bear to even be in the presence of that body any longer.

The questions only really hit him clearly in the car as he guided it home. And with the questions came the tears, tears he had thought some degree of professional detachment would save him from. He wiped his face with a hand and tried not to think, but still, the questions kept forcing their way to the forefront of his mind. Had Troy really killed his beloved son? Had he subsequently committed suicide out of sheer guilt? Or had he given up, seen his life as worthless, blamed for a death he had not perpetrated, given standard police or prison guard treatment in the cell? Was the lack of alcohol even a contributing factor? How much of that time twenty-one years ago had been an influence here? Just what had gone on in that head of his?

He pulled into the driveway and sat there behind the wheel of the car, trying to center himself, the only sounds reaching his ears the ticking of the engine as it cooled down. He knew he should get inside; the need for another drink or two was building up in him like he had never felt before.

He closed his eyes. His mouth was dry, and his brain wanted to relax, wanted to shut out the world. But was alcohol the answer? And with that came another thought: Was this alcohol debate what Troy had gone through every day of his life?

Oh, dear God, Troy again. For with the thoughts of that man came unbidden the final, purple-faced image. His eyes shot open, letting loose a fresh flow of tears.

The movement out of the corner of his eye was fast but stood out in the dark night. A flash of white. A touch of gold. He turned his head sharply, but there was nothing there. What on Earth had that been? His brain was playing tricks on him; now he was seeing the same delusions Troy claimed to have seen on the night he…

"Nathan!" He did not know or care how or why, but his son suddenly filled his thoughts.

He threw the car open and sprinted to the house. He fumbled stupidly with his keys before yanking the front door open and…

"Dad? Dad? Please, Dad, please…"

He banged the door to the front room open.

Blood sprayed up in a sudden fountain of glowing scarlet, adding to the already horrific mess about the place.

"Shit!" he screamed and rushed to Nathan's side. The desk had broken, and the tower of his PC had dropped down so the corner had sliced into his thigh, ripping open a deep, ragged hole.

His son's eyes looked in his direction, but there was no focus to them. "She was… beautiful…" Nathan murmured weakly.

"Oh, shit," Francis groaned as yet another geyser pumped forth. "Shit, shit, shit." Nathan's eyes closed, and the next spurt was a lot less intense than those that had preceded it. "Shit," Francis whispered as Nathan fell limp to the floor beside him. "Oh, Nathan. Shit."

1991

"I can't do this." And with that, one of the hooded figures, the one with the bowed head, moved backward, away from the bag in the center of the human ring, a bag that had fallen silent and almost completely still.

Glances were hurriedly exchanged before a second shrugged his shoulders. "We're not going to go through with it anyway," he said and followed the first.

The faces did not need to be seen to know that confusion now reigned.

"Hang on." A third suddenly broke ranks and chased after them. Three of the other four dropped their eyes, surreptitiously looked at one another, then finally followed the rest.

The final figure, the first to have drawn his knife, remained behind, his eyes fixed on the black plastic-clad object. "Shit," he eventually growled and trudged after the others, leaving just the bag in the poorly lit clearing.

By the time everyone caught up with the first, the light from the braziers was barely a vague glow. "What in the fuck are you doing?" Luke threw his hood back and grabbed the arm of the first one to have left, shaking him.

Francis's hood fell from his head at that. "We can't seriously do this," he hissed. "It's fuckin' insane!" His gaze fell accusingly onto Troy, as the last to leave came close and dropped his cowl.

"But it's for us! It's for our future!" Luke shot back.

"This is just a joke." Francis resumed his march away from the others.

Brandon grabbed his arm. "But it worked once already," he stated.

"Twice," Sean corrected, but his comment went virtually unnoticed amid the heightened emotions.

"I don't care," Francis returned passionately. "A chicken's a chicken, but this…"

Silence fell over them. He was, of course, one hundred percent correct. But another thought entered their minds—they had gone too far already, but was it too far for them to realistically turn back now?

Chapter Seven

2012

Sean opened the door of his house, and Brandon was taken aback by how much weight he had lost in the ten days or so since his son's funeral. "Hi," he croaked, offering Brandon a limp, moist handshake. "Come on in."

"Th-thanks." Brandon simply could not hide his surprise or concern as he followed his old friend inside his large home.

"Can I get you a drink or something?" Sean offered.

"Just a water'll be fine," Brandon replied, looking around at the surroundings. Sean had done well for himself, if the material possessions on display were any indication. They made their way to a dining room, where Sean left him to go through a set of swinging doors into a large kitchen. Instead of taking a seat, Brandon strolled casually around the room, looking at the walls. The pictures and photographs and framed certificates seemed to have been placed at random on the walls, in various positions and at various heights. He looked at one and saw Sean in his gown at his university graduation, and next to that, a slightly overweight woman in similar dress—most likely Sean's wife's own graduation. Then there was a gap and then a picture of a young woman holding a trophy.

He looked closer at the gap. There was a faint yet distinct change in color.

A picture had been removed.

He moved quickly to the next gap and was faced with the same discoloration. And the next, and then three in a row, then two more. A pair of vacant areas stood out amongst the trophies on the mantelpiece. A large area on another wall was empty.

Where were the pictures of Simon?

"You all right in there?" Brandon spun in surprise and caught a glimpse of deep resentment and suspicion cross his old friend's visage.

"Yeah, sure," he smiled, accepting the offered glass. "Thanks."

"So, why'd you come over?" That suspicion was definitely there, deliberately unconcealed.

Brandon smiled as well as he could. "I came over to see how you're doing," he stated softly.

Sean stared at the glass of bourbon and Coke in his hand. "Why so concerned now?" he asked bitterly. "After I transferred my studies, I barely heard from any of you. Hell, I don't even know how you got invites to… to… Oh, Christ." He started to cry then, the sobs running through his whole body in huge spasms, his shoulders heaving as if in physical pain.

Brandon walked carefully to him and placed his hands on the upset man's shoulders. Sean barely acknowledged him. "Can I ask what happened?" he whispered.

"You know how it was a car crash," Sean sniffed, wiping his nose with the back of his hand. "Well, it was worse than that. They said it looked like he swerved to avoid something, slammed into the back of a truck, a sheet of corrugated iron...it went...the window...his head... Oh, for fuck's sake."

Brandon watched uncomfortably for a brief while before patting him on the shoulder. "What about your wife, your daughter?" he forced himself to ask.

He shook his head. "Robyn's staying with Teresa; remember, my sister?" Brandon nodded. "Celeste is... oh, Christ, man, she's been sedated. She's in the hospital, man. It's killing her." He looked at Brandon through puffy eyes. "We lost our youngest at birth, hell, eight years ago. This brought it all up again. We got home from Simon's funeral and Celeste just lost it. She screamed and blamed me and...and...and it was fucking awful. Every single mistake from the past nineteen years was dragged up and thrown in my face." The tears increased. "But you know the only thing I could think of?"

Brandon shook his head, almost afraid to ask.

"Come on. Brandon Cornelius, investigative journalist, surely you can work it out?" Sean was mocking him, something that really did not sit well. *Had the separation been that bad? Which separation?* he suddenly asked himself and shuddered a little.

Brandon's face fell. "Okay, I know," he whispered,

stepping away. "Look, there's no easy way to tell you this," he went on, changing the subject deliberately. "I also came to say that…well…that Troy's dead. He…he hung himself in a holding cell."

Sean's face grew even paler. He tried to speak, but the words wouldn't come out. He fell into a chair, looking like he'd been punched.

"Sean, he killed his son," Brandon muttered, forcing himself to continue. "And Francis's eldest is in the hospital. He might lose his leg."

Sean slumped backward, staring at the wood-paneled ceiling. Then: "Christ, man, what the fuck's going on?" His eyes fell on Brandon, and there was a brand new emotion in them—sheer, unadulterated panic. "It's because of… oh man, it is, isn't it?"

"It can't be," Brandon hissed.

Sean did not reply immediately. He merely finished his drink and let his head drop forward so his eyes caught Brandon's like spotlights. Then: "But it is, right? Simon died on September nineteen—" He swallowed back a fresh bout of tears. "—and doesn't that ring a bell? Doesn't it?" He was sobbing so badly Brandon thought he was going to go into cardiac arrest.

"How can it be?" Brandon finally asked. "It was all bullshit."

"Was it bullshit to Teresa after that accident?" Sean retorted.

Brandon had no response. All he could do was turn and stride out of the house, not once looking back. He just had to get away. Sean's terror was a contagion that had well and truly infected him as well.

1990

"You stole one of their fucking books?" Julian could not believe what Troy had told him.

"No-one noticed," Troy smiled. "Besides, it's old and crappy, and you found your textbook and wrote everything down from that, so it looked like we did what we came to do." The grin turned into a little chuckle. "Once we got to writing, that old fart barely took notice of us. We were just two more nerds who'd come into his lifeline stuck alone in the cellar. Real words, reading and writing. Like we were going to steal anything."

"But if you're going to steal a book, why a useless one from more than a hundred years ago?"

Troy gazed at him seriously. "Knowledge is power. That's what you've been saying. Well, we want power. This—" He held up the book. "—could be something cool."

Julian snatched the book out of Troy's grasp and flicked through its old and fragile pages. His eyes widened as he went, and he shook his head even as his mouth fell open. "Have you lost your fucking mind?" Julian eventually asked incredulously.

"What?"

He held the book up. "Satanic rituals? Seriously?"

"It's worth a go."

"How do you work that out?" Julian felt a wave of all-encompassing anger start to rise.

Troy gazed at him strangely, the smile fading. "*Any-*

thing's worth a go," he stated. "If it fails, then our knowledge is it's shit. But at least we'll know."

"Of course it's going to fucking fail! It's magic, hocus pocus, ooga-booga bullshit!" He paced around. "For fuck's sake, this isn't *Dungeons and Dragons*. This is real fuckin' life!"

"And you know this because?" Troy was now goading him and enjoying himself while doing it, which only served to make Julian more furious.

"Because it's logic! Magic flies in the face of logic!"

"Thank you, Mister Spock."

Julian rolled his eyes. "Look… Listen, it's just a waste of time! It simply won't work! It…"

"Prove it."

Julian opened his mouth to rebuff his friend, but no words came out, until, finally, "I can't prove it; I just know."

Troy's smile suddenly returned. "That's what the priests at school say about God." He laughed. "You don't accept it from them. Why say it now?" He cocked his head and briefly chewed his inner cheek. "And don't tell me you're not curious about this, even a little bit."

Julian just glared at him, feeling like the man who had lost the war in the very first battle.

Chapter Eight

2012

Chantelle stood against the front wall of the night club and groaned. She felt awful—light-headed, nauseous, weak. Her legs struggled to keep her upright, but she knew she couldn't afford to sit down or do anything else. The taste of vomit struck the back of her throat, so she turned and tried to throw up, to get whatever it was out of her system, but to no avail. All it did was make her vision blur and her dizziness increase. It was an effort to even stand steadily but she forced herself to do so. This was not good and getting worse by the minute.

She leaned back against the wall and looked across at the door, where two bouncers were ignoring her plight, instead choosing to deal with two clearly underaged boys who were trying desperately to bluff their way inside.

Her eyes drifted across the road to the multi-story car park that serviced this part of town. Her little Hyundai was parked between two large four-wheel drive vehicles on the third level. She had struggled to get out of the door when she had first arrived, squeezing between her car and a new Toyota, but there was no way she was going to force her way back through that gap in her current state, let alone get the key into the lock.

Something buzzed against her hip. She actually started to relax. She pulled the phone out of her pocket. 'Where r u?' was blinking on the screen under the name "Carmel."

She brought up the screen and tapped in, "sic ouysodi." She scowled, deleted everything, and tried again, taking a lot longer than she would have liked. 'Sick. Im outsid'

The response was not what she'd expected: "Call a cab." She felt the tears welling up. Why was Carmel ignoring her? Why were her friends treating like this? Why…? She shook her head hard. It wasn't Carmel. Whatever this shit in her was, it was messing her up, not only physically, but also emotionally.

She scrolled down her phone's contact list until she found the three-letter word she wanted. She tapped it and held it to her ear. She closed her eyes while she waited, but the colors swimming in what should have been darkness made her open them rapidly.

"Luke Archer speaking." The voice sounded distant to Chantelle's addled mind.

"Dad, it's me." The tears started to flow as soon as she started to talk, an emotion that sounded loud in her words, a warning bell to a doting father.

"Where are you, Shan? What's wrong?" He clearly

could not keep the panic out of his voice.

"At the Down And Out Nightclub." Her words were starting to slur. "Get me?"

"Give me five." She managed a smile as her father disconnected the call. She glanced once more in the direction of the bouncers and saw that somehow the line to get in had grown, giving them even more potential patrons to harass. She debated joining the throng but decided that being sick over there would only lead to more trouble because the vomit was creeping up on her again.

A man stepped out of the hotel, shaking his coat and looking casually across at the high-rise car park. Then he turned his head slowly until his eyes fell on Chantelle.

There was no mistaking his malicious smile, nor the recognition in his eyes. He started towards her, slow at first, but his speed increased, hands opening and closing like the claws of a lobster.

Chantelle stumbled away as quickly as she possibly could on weak, unsteady legs. She reached the edge of the building, used it to turn the corner, and continued on her way before her vision focused enough for her to realize she was heading towards a dead end with just one firmly closed door to greet her. "Oh, shit," she whispered and spun around.

He was already standing there. The grin was wide, revealing broken and rotting teeth punctuated by random gaps. "Come on, honey-bunch," he rasped. "Don't be shy. You won't feel a thing." Then a low laughter followed as he licked his cracked lips with his lizard-like tongue.

"Ge' 'way fru muh," she blurted, her mouth feeling

as though she'd just left a dentist's office.

He continued to approach, the hands opening and closing, opening and closing. She stepped backward, but her legs could no longer hold her weight, and she collapsed to the ground, painfully and abruptly. She tried to push herself, but her arms had lost all their strength, and she fell heavily onto her back.

The man was standing over her before she realized what was happening. He knelt down with a leg on either side of her hips. He let his hands run up her sides and roughly cup her breasts. He squeezed them hard before planting his disgusting mouth on her neck. As he was doing that, he dropped down so that his pelvis rubbed against hers; she felt him grow hard even through the layers of clothing that separated them.

"Nuhh..." she uttered as he moved one of his hands to her pants and forced his fingers down towards the hem of her panties.

"Oh, yes," he growled and lifted his head to look at her.

For the briefest but clearest of moments, the face that stared down at her was female, another delusion caused by whatever the hell had been given her unawares. A beautiful girl, maybe the same age as her, staring at her so sincerely and serenely...and then it was him again, and this time his mouth crushed against her flushed cheek. She squeezed her eyes shut and pursed her lips and swung her head sideways, but he sought her out, trying to latch onto her mouth, moving across her like a snake constricting its prey.

Then he was off her. She heard a solid thud and a loud cry of pain. She risked a peek and saw one of the bouncers standing off to one side, holding her assailant against the wall, the light from a torch showing that the ugly man's face was bloodied, his nose very disfigured and flattened, a swelling under his eye growing even as his feet struggled to reach the ground.

Then: "Shan!"

The bouncer holding the bleeding man turned his head with an almost audible snap, and the torch beam was redirected.

"It's okay. It's okay, mate…"

Chantelle knew that voice. "Da'!" she cried, and then Luke was there. He lifted her head and held her close, and she bawled against his chest, sobs wracking her body, her arms hanging down uselessly.

The bouncer growled and rammed the butt of the torch between his captive's legs, then gave Chantelle a satisfied nod. She tried to smile back.

Suddenly, she turned her face and threw up all over the ground, the regurgitation burning at her throat and mouth. It came out again, and this time it was accompanied by a scream of pain that Chantelle did not realize was coming from her. Then it happened again. Now her ears were filled with the rhythm of blood pumping through her brain; her eyes clouded over completely.

Yet again her stomach spasmed and more was forced out, but there was now little left inside her; she could taste the blood that filled her mouth, even as the searing pain within her filled her body. She desperately sought her father but could not even feel his arms around her. All there was was pain.

And then nothing.

1991

Silence.

It enveloped the seven teenagers sitting on the ground, none of them really sure what was what anymore. What had seemed to be something that should be done now, in the harsh light of reality, just felt so, so…wrong? Terrible? Really fucked up? No. No words could adequately describe the way they felt.

"So, now what?" Julian muttered, his tone a mixture of dejection and anger.

"I guess that's it," Francis said with more hope in his tone than he was aware he was expressing. "We go home." He shrugged. "It's all shit anyway."

"So, why are you here?" Troy demanded.

Francis dropped his eyes, partly in embarrassment, partly in confusion. "I…I didn't want to miss out," he muttered, then threw himself onto his back. "For fuck's sake, is this what we've become? We're smart! We're going to make something of our lives! And we're out here doing something like this? And to her? Following each other like pathetic sheep? Seriously?"

"I know what this is all about," Troy hissed. "You were going to stop us, no matter what. All for her. Un-fucking-believable."

"Like you were really going to do it anyway," Francis countered.

Troy's mouth barely moved. He chewed the inside of his cheek and seethed.

The others all remained silent. They gazed around, but eventually, all eyes returned to the direction of the copse.

"So, what about…you know… Her?" Brandon jerked his thumb where they were all looking.

"Leave her," Troy stated coldly. "We'll call someone to come get her. Call it payback. We just go."

"Payback?" Francis asked.

"What do you mean?" Luke asked carefully.

"Well, I don't care," Troy snarled. "We just go."

"For fuck's sake," Francis muttered.

"She'll know it was all of us," Julian said suddenly. "Don't tell me she doesn't know it was you in the first place." The last comment was directed right at Troy.

He mulled it over in his mind as if this was the first time that thought had even occurred to him. Panic marred his expression. He knew that Julian was, unfortunately, so very correct. Somehow, things had just become worse. "We'll pay her off," Troy said quietly. "Buy her silence. Say it was a joke that got out of hand. We'll get away with it. Her family's rich, but not that rich. She'll take the money, and we'll run."

Eyes fell on Francis.

"Just go?" he repeated.

"Just go." Troy glared at his old friend. "Sorry for you, I guess, but we just fuckin' go."

"Sure," Francis murmured. "Go. Leave it all behind. Why not?"

But, he noted uneasily, not one of them made a move.
Including him.

Chapter Nine

2012

The office door was unimposing, with only the legend "Dr. Worthington" on a faux brass plaque set in the middle of it to indicate whose office it was.

Brandon knocked loudly and then looked around in case he'd disturbed anyone in any of the other rooms.

The door was opened, and Julian stared at him in surprise. He noticed a head appear a little way up the passage. He decided to play this one formally. "Mister Cornelius, good of you to come. Please, come on in," he stated graciously.

"My pleasure," Brandon replied, entering slowly and closing the door behind him.

Julian offered him a seat, and he fell into it. "Shit, look at you," Julian said. "What the hell's wrong now?"

Brandon stared at him for a long, before saying, "I got a call from Luke this morning. His daughter's in hospital. They don't know if she'll make it or not."

All color drained from Julian's face, but he tried to keep his composure. And yet he found he couldn't say anything.

"That leaves you, me, and Randolph," Brandon went on, suddenly and quietly. "Randolph and his wife are already at my place with his kids and my family."

Julian held a hand up. "Why?" he asked.

"Four out of the seven of us. The oldest child each time. You call this coincidence?"

"Yes." His smirk was unintentionally condescending. "You're a writer. You're letting the whole imagination thing get the better of you. You might be a journalist, but I'll bet you're a frustrated novelist. Sorry, mate."

Brandon shook his head. "Even after everything we..."

"Nothing happened!" Julian shot back.

"How can you say that?"

"No, we did what we did, and nothing happened. It was all a sham! Bullshit mumbo-jumbo! We were suckered in because Troy and Sean got lucky."

"Then explain all of this!" Brandon was growing increasingly frustrated. "For God's sake, Troy and Sean lost kids, Troy topped himself, Francis's son got lucky, Luke's daughter is touch and go. What is it going to take?"

"To what?"

"Admit that this is related to something we did, and you know perfectly well there was only one thing we ever did that..." His voice trailed off.

"That what?"

"Deserves revenge," Brandon stated softly, almost sadly, the emotions threatening to break out.

"Revenge? Seriously? Now, after twenty-odd years? Come on, grow up. Troy and Francis were questioned because of all that crap in the uni caf', but it was never serious, and they didn't even bother to talk to the rest of us. And why should they? Academically minded scholars from an elite private school? Shit, by the time they questioned them, Troy was sort of doing that Samantha chick —the one fixated on organic chemistry, remember her?— and we all hardly looked like the sort of desperates who'd do…well…what they guessed had been done. And Francis was a fucking basket-case. He was beside himself. God only knows how he passed that year."

"Then you explain it."

"Coincidence." Brandon opened his mouth to argue, but Julian continued quickly, "Look, it's simple. It's unfortunate, but it's simple: Coincidences happen. Shit happens."

Brandon stood and shook his head. "Well, that's your choice. We're not taking any chances. We're going to watch our kids and keep them watched and do everything we can to keep them safe. *Everything*," he said before striding out of the office.

Julian watched him go. What he had said made no sense. How could normally rational people believe crap like that? It was as bad as high school with the priests forcing their Catholicism down the throats of everyone in their care. Beliefs were crutches, excuses, examples of ignorance. He, on the other hand, knew. And his knowledge was more important and more powerful than anyone's belief.

Especially a two-decades-old piece of adolescent fuck-wittery that they had all paid for a thousand times in their dreams.

1990

Troy stood at the wooden block and looked at the other two with him. He opened the old book and read the words within with a practiced ease borne of too many years of exposure to Latin. Randolph and Luke exchanged glances but said nothing; this was Troy's baby, Troy's idea, and, if anything was to come of it, Troy's good fortune.

They were here out of curiosity and a sense of friendship that Troy's fervor was making them both think was incredibly misguided.

Then he slid out from the back of his pants a long, thin-bladed knife, the metal etched with three markings that stood out; Luke recognized them as the Greek letters theta, eta, and omicron. Troy held this up with both hands as if offering a child up for baptism and proffered a long string of Latin, spoken quickly and fluently.

Then he grabbed a bag lying behind the block and lifted it carefully. He opened it and removed a chicken; its beak, wings, and legs were all bound, yet still, it struggled for release. The band on its leg told the other two this was one of the pets from Troy's own backyard. He laid the bird on the block and raised the knife. Then he screamed, "My greatest desire is to have more money!"

And with those words, he drove the point of the dagger into the back of the helpless animal, right between the wings. The blood sprayed up, and it struggled more strongly, yet futilely, against its bonds. Troy looked at the book one last time, nodded to himself, and then lifted the chicken and bit into its neck, wrenching his head back and forth until the animal's throat came out in an eruption of red. He turned and spat out the hunk of flesh and errant feathers, then grinned at the other two, blood staining his mouth, his eyes maniacal, his muscles tense and on edge.

He looked as much like an animal as any man Luke or Randolph had ever seen before. And both of them were terrified.

Chapter Ten

2012

Francis pulled the wheelchair in through the double doors and paused.

Luke peered up from his bedside vigil with all the world-weariness of a man who had refused to sleep, but even on seeing who his visitors were, he could not force so much as a half-smile onto the corners of his mouth.

"Hey," Francis said quietly. "How is she?"

Luke shrugged, but that was all it took for the crying to start. "They still don't know," he muttered. "Whatever she was given burnt her stomach, right through her stomach. The acids got out and... and... oh, shit, man, she's in a real bad way."

Francis pushed the chair to the bed and looked at the girl. Her hair, slightly longer than shoulder length, was unbound and spread messily across the pillow. Her cheeks were sunken, her color ashen. Tubes ran into her nose and mouth, intravenous drips into the crooks of both elbows. A heart monitor beside her bed told the world that her heart rate was a steady but low fifty-eight beats per minute, while her blood pressure also was not strong.

"And who's this?" Luke asked, seeming to notice the wheelchair for the first time.

"Oh, Luke Archer, meet my son Nathan," Francis said, then snorted a humorless laugh. "It's about time our kids met, I reckon."

"Wish it could have been under better circumstances," Luke mumbled, stroking his daughter's head absently.

Nathan leaned forward, his bandaged leg restricting the movement. He did not show any discomfort, and Francis could not tell if that was a deliberate ploy or if his desire to play football again was pushing him through everything. "This is Chantelle," Francis said, "and this is her father, Luke, one of my old high school friends."

Nathan watched the girl on the bed for a long time, then asked almost nervously, "If you were such good friends, why haven't we met before?"

Luke and Francis cast one another sad glances before Francis placed his hand on his son's shoulder. "Sometimes things happen when we're kids. People grow apart. Lives change. That's all," he explained.

"But mum didn't even know about these guys."

Francis grimaced. "Well, looking at it, I guess I lost contact with everyone at the end of first-year university. Your mum and I didn't meet until I started work at Winston and Carruthers when I was in third year." Nathan knew the rest of the story—his mum got pregnant, they got married, his dad finished his studies, and now here they were. It all seemed a world away from a group of seven friends living out of one another's pockets.

"We've sort of kept up with what each other's been doing," Luke added. "And Brandon's kept tabs on all our contact details. That's how we found out about Sean, and Simon's funeral." His voice faltered on those final words, and he subconsciously shifted his hand to Chantelle's cheek.

Silence fell over them like a stifling cloud, and Nathan took the opportunity to look at Chantelle again. "I hope she pulls through," he said absently, more to himself than the others. He settled back on the wheelchair and subconsciously rubbed his leg but found the other two staring at him. "What?" he asked defensively.

Francis smiled. "She's only a year older than you, you know," he said, trying for the sort of embarrassing joke they had often shared over the years.

Nathan gave him a look of mock disdain but could not help but return his gaze to the young woman in the bed. "Why us?" he asked quietly.

All traces of humor disappeared from the faces of the older men.

That was not a question either of them wanted to think about.

1991

Troy stood first and looked at the rest. "Yep, that's right. I suppose we should just let her go," he muttered. He pulled the book out from under his robes and gazed at it with a deep sense of longing. The others could all feel it. He had actually done this before; he knew exactly what was at stake here. Luke and Randolph had seen it, had seen the blood, had seen the animal their friend had become.

All of them had seen the results.

And one of them, unbeknownst to the others, had been inspired in the face of tragedy, had also witnessed it first-hand, had seen the power, was sure of its truth.

But all of them had noted that there had been something different about Troy ever since that afternoon…

Troy headed back toward the small clearing, the book held before him as though it was made of precious gemstones, a religious icon to be revered.

Sean was the one who followed him, knowing all too well just what they were giving up, then, one by one, the others all stood and shuffled away until only Francis was left. He closed his eyes and shook his head. They didn't need him there. They would open the bag, untie her and simply leave her be, freezing cold in that flowing white nightdress that Troy had forced her to wear. Then they would return and everyone would go home, and they would live with this shame for the rest of their lives.

He fought the tears that threatened to overwhelm him. What in God's name had they been thinking when they had come here? Hell, what in God's name had they been thinking when they had even decided to try this? To that point, what had he been thinking when, at the last moment, he had agreed to accompany them? This was not like them at all. But it must have been because, well, here they were.

Even him.

Power; all for power. Power and influence and the world on their terms.

How stupid was that?

It had become an obsession with them, the seven of them, even himself, he had to admit. Ever since that day with the control they found they could wield over a moron footballer, it had become a deep obsession: anything they could learn about anything—or anyone—that was out of the ordinary, just to increase the power they felt they were owed, to change the world into the vision they had for it, and then when university had been so different, they wanted that high school power back, they wanted everything under their control.

And why? Some form of petty revenge against a world they thought had ignored them unjustly? Was that it?

He felt physically ill.

And the thought of going back to university tomorrow, just another Friday, made him feel even worse.

And she barely entered his thoughts. After everything else, he was not thinking about her...

"Uhh, I think we've got a problem."

Francis looked up with a start and saw Julian standing there. He didn't need to ask any questions; the look on his friend's face said it all.

This had somehow gone from incredibly bad to even worse.

Chapter Eleven

2012

"Look, this can't be anything to do with what happened," Julian stated bluntly. "She was never found. We weren't…"

"Then why us and why now?" Luke shot back. "There has to be a connection."

"Why?" Julian stood and leaned on the table, his cigarette clenched between his teeth. His eyes fell on Brandon, who had arranged this gathering in the private room at the hotel Francis frequented.

"Our kids, man," Sean whispered. "Look at our fuckin' kids. And who's to say it'll stop with just the oldest one for each of us? What if that's just the start? Oh, shit, what if…"

"For God's sake, this is all just coincidence!" Julian cried. "Some nasty accidents have happened, sure, but these things happen. There is no-one out there out to get us through our children."

"I did some digging," Brandon stated suddenly, taking out a notebook. "Her father died about a year later, heart attack, but the newspaper wrote it up as a broken heart," he read, "and her mother now lives in New Zealand, remarried. Her younger brother is, get ready for this, currently a teacher at our old high school, but he's actually changed his surname, probably because of everything that's happened. That's a strong connection between him and Francis's and Julian's kids, who all go there. Her youngest sister is married to a…"

"Hang on, hang on, you're looking for fucking suspects now?" Julian exploded. "This is just as insane as that whole thing was back then. We're dealing with insanity by being insane now? What the hell is this?"

"My daughter's in the fucking hospital with a fucking hole in her stomach!" Luke screamed passionately. "Don't you dare tell me this is all insane! Don't you dare! I'm living with this insanity every single, fucking day. We have to find who's doing this. Shit, Randolph won't even leave his son's side. And look what happened to Troy. We have to stop it! I don't care how—we have to stop it. Please." Tears poured down his face. "You should see her," he eventually went on, his voice struggling, the words being forced out. "She's so helpless, lying there, and we don't know if she's going to come out of it or not." He wiped his face with his sleeve, like the school boy he felt he was once more. "And there's not a thing we can do."

Silence fell over them, none comfortable enough after so long apart to comfort Luke, but none willing to abandon him. Even Francis hesitated awkwardly. The years that had once flown away suddenly weighed heavily on them all.

Glances were exchanged, drinks were sipped, Julian crushed his cigarette into oblivion in an ashtray, but that was all. The atmosphere grew thicker, and the four men felt like slowly moving away from one another, inch by inch.

"Thunderstruck" suddenly sounded out, and Francis fumbled with his pocket while the others all looked relieved that something had broken the tension.

He looked at the number on the screen, shrugged, then held it to his ear. "Francis Coulter speaking," he stated mechanically. He paused, but the bored expression he affected quickly became one of shock and disbelief. His mouth fell open, and he squeezed his eyes shut. "What do you...?" he mumbled, wiping his hand over his face with force. "Say, ten, fifteen minutes?" He looked at Julian suddenly. "Sure, I'll make sure he comes along. How is..." He closed his eyes again. "See you there," he muttered before staring at his phone as though that would change everything that had just happened.

"What?" Julian asked, but he sounded as if he already knew the answer.

"That, that was Randy," Francis muttered. "It's... oh, God. Guys, it's Eric, his son. He's... he's in the hospital. I don't know all the details," he added quickly, "but, oh shit, it's not good." Stunned expressions greeted this announcement. Even in high school, they had considered Randolph the least of their "Round Table," the one who hadn't quite fit in anywhere else, who had struggled most with education, and then who had been the first to break off all contact with the others at the end of their first year of university. But he was still one of them and always would be. Francis finally continued, softly, with concern, "He wants me to go to the hospital. Me and..."

"Me," Julian sighed. He looked near tears. "I should've been there," he whispered. "For all those years, I should have been there. Where was I?"

"Look, Randolph was the one who made the choice to cut all his ties with us," Francis stated as calmly as he could manage. "He dropped out of uni, took that apprenticeship, moved out of home, didn't return phone calls. Even his parents were worried about him. You can't blame yourself." He shook his head. "But that was then and this is now. And now he wants his best friend there." His gaze returned to Julian. "That's you, mate."

A single, choked sob escaped Julian's lips before he lit a cigarette with a shaking hand, grabbed his jacket, and made his way from the room. Francis watched him go, then muttered to the rest, "Follow us."

They didn't need to be asked twice.

1990

Francis and Julian climbed out of Julian's car in the student car park, both using the side mirrors to ensure their uniforms were neat and tidy. "Hiya!" Luke called from his car, swinging his over-laden schoolbag onto his shoulder.

"Hey!" Francis returned with a nod of his head. He then gazed across at the three figures approaching from the direction of the school buildings. "What's going on?" he asked.

Luke shrugged as he reached the other two, watching the trio comes toward them. "What's up?" he asked when they finally reached them.

"Troy asked us to meet him here," Sean explained. "We all caught the early bus to make sure we were here."

"Hey, he rang me last night as well," Luke said, "but I was at chess club. Mum said he didn't leave a message. Any idea what this is all about?"

"None whatsoever," Sean muttered as they watched a pair of motorcycles roar past. The two riders and one pillion passenger ignored them as they parked in the designated area.

"So where do we go?" Francis asked.

"He said to meet here, at Julian's car," Brandon said with a shrug. He sat on the front of the vehicle casually. "So, I guess we wait. But I reckon he must have his shit-box V-Dub on the road, wants to show it off or something."

"Sounds about right," Luke snorted. Bags were then dropped, and they relaxed and waited. Troy did not come from a wealthy background—his grandparents paid his tuition fees—and the rest of them indulged his little shows of pride with something that could well have been recognized as condescension if they had been more self-aware.

"Stoney's got a new car," Luke said with a nod as a silver Saab pulled into the lot.

"Nice one, too," Sean muttered. "Wish my old man owned a car yard."

"Instead of being a physiotherapist? Yeah, right," laughed Brandon. "But, hey, you could get one like Sergio's." He pointed at the next car arriving at the school, a green Fiat Bambino with orange panels on the passenger side. They all laughed, a sound that grew louder as they watched their grossly overweight classmate extract himself from behind the steering wheel.

A honking horn distracted them. They turned and watched in silence as a new EA Ford Falcon six-cylinder pulled slowly into the spot beside Julian's car. The dark blue paint job caught the morning sun with a slight sheen while the tinted windows didn't allow them to see inside.

Then the driver's side door opened and Troy lifted himself up like a Formula One driver after winning a race, grinning at them like the Cheshire Cat. "Like it?" he asked.

"How did you…?"

"What?"

"But you…"

The words came from his friends in a fast and furious onslaught, until he pulled his bag out and locked the vehicle, checking it twice.

"It worked," he stated simply, the smile never leaving his face.

"What? I don't understand…" Francis started, but Randolph stopped him with a hand on the chest. Everyone looked at him expectantly; this was not like him at all, to step forward like this.

"That fuckin' thing with your pet chicken worked?" Randolph hissed incredulously. He was also angry, but the others could not understand why.

"A week ago, I won on a lottery ticket." Somehow, Troy's grin widened. "I got money! Just what I wanted, what I truly desired!"

"It… It worked?" Luke echoed. The others didn't know what to say. They'd heard what had happened, but it had all seemed like some sort of stupid crap that kids their age, exposed to an overload of religiosity, tried every so often to rebel against their staid status quo. Something stupid that meant nothing and would go on to become a great drinking story when they got older, that was all.

But, apparently, no, it wasn't all.

A cold wind blew across the car park. As one of them would later say, shit just got real.

Chapter Twelve

2012

Five men sat in the waiting room of the hospital, drinking a beverage the vending machine called coffee, not speaking, not even looking at one another. The nurse watching the scene from behind a glass barricade was amazed when later informed that these men had been best friends in high school; she had them pegged as mere acquaintances, maybe extended family members at a stretch.

A doctor stood in a doorway and nodded once. Francis and Julian stood and followed him out of the room. The others watched them go as if they were headed to their execution.

They stayed that way, eyes on the closed door, still unable to bring themselves to say anything.

Finally, Luke stood, dropping the half-full cup of coffee in a nearby bin. "Where you going?" Sean muttered.

Luke looked at him and suddenly started. In the

sterile environs and harsh lighting, Sean looked like he had aged more than the mere two decades they had been estranged. A quick glance at Brandon gave him a similar impression; he dreaded to think how he appeared to them. "I'm going to check in with my wife and daughter," he stated, distraught at how thick his tongue felt.

He didn't wait for a response as he trudged to the stairs and took them like a drunk man until he was at the appropriate floor. Without looking at any of the staff, he followed a path he had come to know way too well in such a short time.

He slowed as he reached the door of the room. His wife was sitting in one of the cold, hard chairs in the corridor, her shaking hands holding a can of soda. "Annie, what's wrong?" He peered sideways nervously. "Is Shan all right? Is everything okay? Is…?"

"I just needed a break, calm down," Annalise muttered. "Chantelle's okay. Well, the same as…you know." Her thin grasp on her emotions almost faltered, her bottom lip quivering, but somehow she kept herself from tipping over the edge into a complete breakdown.

"Is anyone in there with her?" Luke's panic made Annalise wince, guilt momentarily marring her expression.

It took a few moments of staring at the can, its contents barely touched, for the woman to be able to proceed. "Yes," she murmured, the hint of a smile touching her mouth. "In fact, he's been in with her since they served dinner."

"Who? A doctor? An intern?" The panic was slowly turning to terror. "Has she taken a turn for the worse?"

Annalise stood quickly and gripped him by the arms. "Don't… Just don't," she whispered. "You… You need to be strong. For Chantelle." She fell against him. "For me. Please."

"I don't understand…" he started, but she was shaking her head straight away.

"No, no, you don't." She jerked her head at the door. "Have a look."

Luke moved away from her and looked through the window in the door. "Him?" he whispered.

"I met his father this morning as well. Another old high school friend, another good friend I knew nothing about." She seemed to consider her words before finally asking, "What's going on here?"

Luke just looked at Nathan, sitting in his wheelchair, reading aloud from a thick book to the unconscious girl in the bed. "I don't know what's going on," he answered distractedly. "And what is he doing in there?"

"What's he doing? Something both of us should have been doing." She shook her head. "He asked me what her favorite book is and—you know something?—I didn't know." The tears started again. "She's nineteen years old, she's in her first year of university, and I didn't even know the name of her favorite damn book! I had to send Eloise a message." Her mouth curled into a cruel half-smile. "I saw that look on your face just then. You don't even know who Eloise is."

"Well, I guess it's a friend," he tried.

"Try her best friend." Annalise shook her head sadly. "She's her best friend." Her voice dropped low and quavered again.

"I thought that was Vi." Luke could not believe he was having this conversation here, with his daughter lying in what he could only think of as a coma, and with a group of friends he had not seen for around twenty years gathered two floors below, where one was going through the exact same thing as him with his son.

"She went to Korea for a family emergency and decided to stay. That was almost eighteen months ago," Annalise sighed, breaking into his train of thought abruptly and starkly.

Luke looked through the window once more. "So, what's he reading to her?" he asked.

"*Twilight.*" Annalise joined him. "Nice kid, that one. When he found out what the book was, he looked horrified, and I thought he'd just say, 'Forget it.' But he said he'd do it."

"Why?"

She shrugged. "He said it'd be good for her and he knew how hard it'd be for us, so he just said he'd do it." She moved away and sat once more, this time taking a mouthful from the can. "He's a good one. Nice guy. I think he's really doing it to keep his own mind off everything that's happening—something about not being able to play football or something?—but he's still doing it, and for a girl he's never met."

"Just like his old man," Luke mumbled, unable to take his eyes from the scene playing out before him. "A real nice guy."

A beep came from his pocket, and he absently pulled

the phone from his pocket. He stared at the screen. His face went instantly pale.

"What is it?" Annalise asked urgently, yet carefully.

Luke held up the phone. The single word message was enough to make Annalise's tears flow more freely.

"Shit."

***

Luke slowed down only as he came to the door where a concerned-looking nurse let him enter. Randolph was crouched beside an empty bed, his hands balled into tight fists, his face buried into a sheet that hung over the side. Julian was beside him, a hand on his shoulder, looking completely lost and helpless. Luke joined the other three, standing off to one side, but he found he could not stay there for long. Especially not when he overheard one nurse whisper to another, "What would make a twelve-year-old kid slash his wrists like that? What sort of guy is that fa...?" She stopped when she realized Luke was listening, then hastened away in embarrassment.

But, Luke reasoned, at least a part of that was a reasonable question: Why had Eric LeCroix committed suicide, and why now? He found he could not help but gaze up at the ceiling where, somewhere above him, his own daughter was hopefully hearing Francis's son reading to her in her long sleep.

Julian was wrong. This was not a coincidence. He cast a last glance into the room as he stood in the doorway, where Francis and Brandon met his gaze.

They knew.

Definitely not a coincidence, not at all.

1991

Francis could see immediately why the others were so panicked.

One of them had used the point of one of the ornate knives Troy had managed to procure—none asked how or where from—to undo the zip along the top of the bag, as if actually physically touching it was going to be too much to bear. The duct tape had been peeled from her mouth and dropped on the ground, but that only made it seem worse.

Chelsea's lips were blue, her eyes closed, her skin almost a translucent white except for the deep red of her flushed cheeks.

Francis looked wildly about. "Is she...?" he started.

Troy turned his back on them all.

"I couldn't feel a pulse," Sean whimpered pathetically.

Francis knelt down beside the still body and pushed his cold fingers against her carotid artery. He felt a chill run up his spine, making the hairs on his neck stand on end and goose-pimples break out all over his body. He bent down to press his ear against her mouth. He pushed himself closer and closer, crushing his cheek against her face harder and harder.

Without saying anything, he gripped her nose and chin and tilted her head back, opening her mouth and breathed down her throat, watching to make sure her chest rose. Five times, then he switched, and in the center of her sternum, he pumped with the heels of his hands before returning to the mouth, a mouth he had kissed so often in the past, and yet which he was now trying to use to save her life. Breathe, pump, breathe pump... he could not stop.

The others watched this ritual with fearful detachment before Troy gathered the courage to mumble, "Considering what we were going to do, this is sort of..."

A sharp elbow to his ribs from Brandon silenced him, and the looks Troy received from all the others were accusing and guilty, tacitly telling him that, of course, they weren't going to go through with his crazy plans.

Of course not.

Gazes were once more returned to Francis's frantic efforts on the ground; their thoughts were solely and fervently hoping he was going to be successful.

Chapter Thirteen

2012

It was paranoia, and only paranoia, that saved the life of Karyn Worthington.

At least, that was how Julian saw it.

But…

Julian sat behind his desk, not focusing on a laboratory report in front of him, written by one of his undergrad students but that he was sure he'd seen somewhere before. If he could prove it, the plagiarism charge would finally get rid of this kid and maybe make some of his so-called mates reconsider doing his subjects. Fresh out of one of the elite private schools—not Julian's old *alma mater*, thank goodness—and with that air of entitlement that he was growing unfortunately accustomed to from those children.

And which he now recognized as having been alive and well in himself and his friends when they had first come here.

His phone beeped, and he grabbed it from the desk beside him. "Can i go 2 Hannah hous?" the message read. Then another beep and the word, "Pleez?" appeared on the screen.

He stared at it, unsure just why he should suddenly feel so uneasy about something that had happened more than two dozen times this year alone. The two of them would get together under the pretense of doing their homework, and then spend the whole time making lip-sync music videos that he wouldn't know about until he checked out the HanKan97 YouTube channel, normally at the instigation of Karyn's younger brother, Brock, as he tried to get his sibling into trouble yet again.

Especially after that "Milkshake" video they did.

No, that wasn't the cause of the uneasiness. The songs Karyn had been incessantly singing just recently were a little older—Kylie Minogue hits from the 1980s and 1990s, of all things, after Hannah's sister had received a greatest video hits DVD of the Australian songstress for her birthday—and that was most likely going to be the current source of their inspiration.

This was crazy. Why was he obsessing about something so pathetic and minor?

He slowly stood, dropping the submitted paper to the top of the pile. That could wait. Whatever was on his mind was growing, and he could not concentrate.

No, there was no "whatever" on his mind. It was Karyn. Not Brock, not his wife, not his work, not his old friends, but Karyn. He stared at the messages again, then, before he could think about it, typed in, "Sure."

He subconsciously grabbed his satchel and slung it over his shoulder.

A third beep. "Thanx dad ur d BEST!" He smiled and locked his office behind him as he left the building.

Without looking where he was going, he scrolled through the apps on his phone and hit the Facebook icon. His page came up on the small screen, and he quickly brought up his family list. He tapped on Karyn's profile picture—taken the previous year with her face painted to look like a zombie—and watched as his daughter's page came up.

"Kickin' it old skool!" read the latest post with a link to the YouTube video of Kylie Minogue's "I Should Be So Lucky."

He reached the bottom of the stairs as a new photo appeared—his daughter and her best friend sitting on the bus in their school uniforms, their long hair swept up into side ponytails, the caption reading, "Ready 4 the 80s!" Still on the bus; that was good... wasn't it?

He strode briskly towards the staff car park, ignoring the incessant chatter of the students milling all around.

Another update—a three-second video on her Vine feed of the two of them singing off-key in the standard selfie pose, though, thankfully, without the ubiquitous duck-face. He smiled as he slid behind the wheel of the car, sticking a cigarette in his mouth and lighting it without so much as a second thought.

He stopped short, holding the key in his hands over the ignition. What was he doing? Without even really thinking about what he was doing, he had left work and climbed into his car, fully prepared to go and get his daughter.

She would probably never forgive him, no matter what excuse he came up with.

He closed his eyes even as he started the engine.

He couldn't help it; he had to keep going.

He plugged the phone into the car as he pulled out onto the road and headed east. The phone suddenly connected automatically as someone rang, the voice cutting in on the car's speakers. "Uhh, hello?" It was a male, exhausted and yet familiar to Julian's distracted mind.

"Yeah, Doctor Worthington speaking," he said mechanically, stubbing his cigarette out.

"This is Francis." There was a touch of relief to the voice.

"Hey, how are you?"

"Good. Actually, real good." He paused. "Chantelle, Luke's kid, just got out of surgery. She had a real bad turn this morning while Nate was with her." Even over the phone's poor connection, his inhalation of breath sounded deep; Julian knew now wasn't the time to interrupt. "She's pulled through. They think she might even finally regain consciousness in the next day or so. But the signs are so much better than before. They apparently missed a hole last time, so they went back in and repaired it. It's finally looking good."

"Thank God! Good news." Julian felt the smile creep across his face, and he shoved another cigarette in and lit it straight away. "How's Luke?"

"Yeah, good, good," Francis chuckled. "Nathan's

in there with them now, but I thought I'd just let you guys know what's going on."

Julian paused before asking the next question. "And how's Randy?"

"Yeah, well, yeah." An icon flashed on the screen, and now Julian just wanted him to hurry; already, Karyn was posting things from Hannah's house. "I'll be seeing him in around forty minutes."

"What do you mean?" A sense of dread hit him, hard and suddenly.

"The police are saying now they don't think Eric meant to commit suicide." Francis's voice took on a distinctly professional tone all of a sudden.

"What? But they found Eric in the shower, didn't they?" This was taking in the definite feeling of a dream. Good news, bad news—and all concerning his old friends.

"Yeah," Francis went on, breaking into his contemplations. "Randolph said he made sure Eric got into the shower okay, and then went to check on him when he thought he'd been in there for too long, even for Eric." He tried to laugh, but it was a hollow sound, made worse by the distance over the telephone. "Anyway, they didn't say Randolph slashed Eric's wrists or anything—at least, not as far as they indicated to me—but that he was aware of Eric's intentions and deliberately delayed going to him."

"That's fuckin' insane!" Julian almost swerved out of his lane as he thumped the steering wheel in anger and frustration. Weren't things bad enough without this as well?

"Yeah, well, that's what I'll be saying. But you can imagine what it's doing to him. First, his son, then this."

"Oh, Christ, I hope he doesn't do, doesn't...you know—Troy," Julian managed.

"That's what I'm afraid of, too." He sighed, a noise that sounded almost frivolous over the phone. "But, look, good news—it seems Chantelle's going to be fine. Let me deal with Randolph." He paused. "For now. But he is going to need your support, too."

Julian swung off the main road. "Yeah, sure, I understand. And thanks for letting us know."

"No problem." A brief, stupidly uncomfortable pause followed, then: "Catch ya later."

"Let me know how things go with Randolph, okay? Or better yet, see if you can get him to call me."

"Will do."

"See ya." He pressed the button to disconnect the call and concentrated on guiding the car the rest of the way to Hannah's house.

He parked across the road two houses down, not really sure what he was doing, and lit yet another cigarette. As he stared at his daughter's Facebook page, a new photo came up. "The STAGE," she had written beneath a photo of what looked like two card tables covered in old bedsheets. He grimaced; she surely couldn't be serious.

Another update, another video, this one from Hannah's Tout account: the two of them sitting on the makeshift stage. "Almost ready," Hannah said, her high-pitched voice grating on Julian as it always had and most likely always would.

"We're going to get dressed and then—video time!" Karyn laughed. Julian had trouble seeing the fifteen-year-old there; he could only remember the six-year-old who wanted so badly to do ballet and yet had run screaming from the stage on the night of her first recital.

A flash of white appeared between them.

"See you in fifteen, peeps!" Hannah squealed.

"HanKan97 on YouTube!" were Karyn's parting words before the video stopped.

Julian laughed a little under his breath, but his sense of panic had increased. He replayed the video. There was something about that flash of white...

He paused it, went through it at the equivalent of frame by frame.

It was one frame only.

A face surrounded by gold and white. Blurred. Fast. Bright.

Terrifying.

He left the car and walked quickly to the front door of the house, crushing the cigarette underfoot as he went. He didn't hesitate before knocking. "Doctor W!" Hannah's mother greeted. "What brings you here?"

He smiled sweetly. "It's a surprise, Tanya," he whispered conspiratorially. "I wanted to watch them make their video." Her expression indicated she believed him completely and wholly. And why wouldn't she? He was Dr. Julian Worthington, professor of applied and theoretical physics, father of Karyn, who was dux of her year level at school, his old school, now co-educational from reception through, unlike when he had been a student there. The school where his old friend's son was School Captain…and he suddenly realized that the surnames had never connected with him before. No, that didn't matter now. What mattered was that he was here and had just lied to Hannah's mother.

Tanya giggled, ushering him in, breaking into his thoughts. "I do that a lot. Come on, they'll be starting soon."

She led him to the large back shed and slid the bolt on a side door, which she opened a crack. It was more a junk room than anything else, though it had probably started its existence as the workshop of Hannah's surgeon father before work took over his life, as it did to them all. Tools were scattered everywhere, with half a motorbike in one corner, an old hoist attached to the roof, and boxes and crates of all sorts of objects piled up everywhere. The girls had set up their stage in the middle of a space they had apparently cleared themselves. The video camera was hooked up to a laptop and rested on top of a pallet of empty bottles, a half-deconstructed wooden bookcase between it and the stage.

"Here they come," Tanya whispered. The front door slid open, and the two girls rushed in. Both were wearing hot pants, which made Julian scowl a little, and tight, long-sleeved tops that showed just how pre-pubescent they really were. But he stayed his ground.

They spoke in hushed tones, then Hannah fiddled with the computer and camera before they climbed onto the tables, both of which shook uneasily as they gained their balance. The music started, and they performed their synchronized dance moves with the biggest grins imaginable on their faces. Julian could not remember the last time he had seen his eldest child having so much fun.

That very thought made him choke up a little.

It hit him.

A definite flash of white.

Julian was moving even before they had landed their jump that had turned them side-on to the camera.

The leg of the table collapsed.

Julian leaped forward.

Karyn didn't get a chance to scream as she tumbled sideways.

Julian's arms stretched out desperately, his eyes never leaving his daughter's falling body.

Her head slammed into his upper arm, driving the limb down and impaling the shoulder muscle on a trio of six-inch nails sticking out of the old bookcase, right where the side of Karyn's chest and the top of her shoulder would have been. His other arm wrapped around her, and he dragged her in close even as he cried out in agony. Karyn screamed in terror and pain, her face cracking against her father's arm and jaw on the rebound. The impact drew blood from her nose and mouth and created a swelling under her eye that ballooned straight away.

And Kylie Minogue's nasal voice continued to croon about how she should be so lucky, lucky, lucky, lucky…

1990

Francis walked slowly out of the school hall and

stretched his body, trying to increase blood flow to his lower extremities after sitting at a small desk for three hours without a break. His head ached a little, but he was happy and more than merely satisfied with his afternoon's work.

"Hey, how'd you go?" came from behind him. He turned and smiled at Troy, who was following him outside.

"Yeah, pretty good, I think," he nodded before breaking into a broad smile. "One more exam to go, then that's that. No more high school."

"I've got two more to go, but, yeah—it's so close I can taste it!" Troy agreed. He sounded exhausted, like every other person in their year level.

They continued to move casually away from the hall, like all the other students filing out. Three hours of reading and writing continuously in complete silence, recalling dates and names, regurgitating a year's worth of knowledge, writing essays—everything a final examination was dreaded to be.

"Franky!" Both of them turned with a start and watched as a stunningly gorgeous girl jogged towards them. She beamed as she sidled up to Francis and kissed him on the cheek. "Thank you," she said, her voice sincere, her smile completely genuine, and all for him.

Troy was stunned. What was Chelsea Hartog, the most desirable and beautiful girl he had ever seen, doing with Francis, destined to be Dux of the school, king of the nerds? A twinge of jealousy rose abruptly in the pit of his stomach.

"So, you did well?" Francis was asking her, her

beauty clearly the only thing he was seeing.

"Oh, hell yeah," she giggled, nodding and moving slightly so she now stood between Francis and Troy so that the only one of the duo in her line of sight was the boy she was talking to, shutting Troy out completely and effectively. This meant all he could see was her hair, gold in color, unbound and hanging down, styled like Christie Brinkley in Billy Joel's "Uptown Girl" video, only longer. His eyes drifted down the sun-yellow tresses to the narrow waist and rounded hips until they rested on her buttocks and the long legs that were barely hidden by the school dress she wore, as short as the rules could possibly allow.

"Got it all done?" Francis went on, ignoring his friend as effectually as the girl he was talking to.

She giggled again, the sound music to the ears of both boys. "Done and dusted with enough time to go over the essay." She grabbed him in a tight embrace around the neck. After a moment's hesitation, he responded in kind, gripping her about the waist, crushing her body against his. She pulled her head back and kissed him lightly on the lips, and they let go simultaneously and gazed at one another, smiling. "Thank you," she purred.

He shrugged, his face reddening in embarrassment. "It was my pleasure," he managed. "Really."

"I still don't really get why." She looked at him curiously. "I mean, you didn't have to." She bowed her head a little. "I thought you wanted to get down my pants, but you didn't even make a move on me like I reckon half the other guys would have done. And virtually no-one knew, so it wasn't even to make yourself look good. I still don't get it." Her eyes darted across to where two other girls were watching with some degree of confusion. "You didn't help Jazz or Sophe."

"You looked like you actually wanted to do well, like you meant it, so I offered to help," he suggested lamely. "And then you didn't treat me like shit, like some of, well…you know, so, well, here we are." He fumbled over his words, feeling more and more embarrassed as he went on.

"No, it was…" She kissed him again. "Thank you." She started to move away, then looked back at him, once more making sure Troy was not in her field of vision. "Oh, you decided if you're coming Saturday?"

He smiled sadly and shook his head. "I'd love to, but I somehow don't think I'd be too welcome."

Her eyes darted in the direction of her friends, but her body did not indicate the fact. "I understand," she said quietly. "And you will be invited to my birthday party in January, which I expect you to make an appearance at. But I still owe you."

"Tell you what," he replied, "when we're at uni together next year, I'll let you buy the coffee."

"It's a date," she laughed, then strode quickly away to join her companions, both Francis and Troy watching her hair swing from side to side in perfect time with her well-shaped hips.

"So, you gonna tell me what that was all about?" Troy eventually asked.

"I told you I've been tutoring some of our classmates," Francis replied dismissively.

Troy dragged his attention from the girl in question. "But Chelsea Hartog? Seriously?"

He shrugged. "So? She said she needed help. So, European history, maths, and biology, I helped her."

"You helped her." Troy's smile became sly. "What did you really get out of it?"

Francis faced Troy and placed a hand on his shoulder. "I got a friend," he stated simply.

Words failed Troy, but that horrid feeling returned to the pit of his stomach. Chelsea Hartog, the girl they had perved on so often in the female toilets, the girl he had followed home too often, the girl of his dreams… the girl who had rebuffed him so crudely not long after his lottery windfall. Of course, Francis and the others knew nothing of that. And he suddenly understood that, really, her rudeness and complete disregard for him had done nothing to diminish what he felt for her. Nor diminish the intense jealousy he felt now.

Nor lessen the fact that he still really, truly wanted her.

And his mind turned to a century-old book sitting even now inside a hollowed-out copy of *Great European Train Journeys* in one of his bookcases.

He smiled humorlessly to himself and followed Francis in silence to the car park.

Chapter Fourteen

2012

Brandon handed Julian a cup of coffee and sat down opposite him, trying desperately to wake up. The clock on the microwave reminded him that it was, indeed, almost quarter past two in the morning, but he tried unsuccessfully to think of this as just a very dark afternoon.

"Thanks," Julian muttered, "and sorry again for waking you up."

"No worries. I had to get up in four hours anyway," he replied deadpan, and then smiled.

"Yeah, well, sorry." The humor didn't touch him. He sat back and gingerly rubbed his shoulder, the sling stopping the arm within it from sagging down too much. "Just so you know, I discharged myself from the hospital and came right here."

"So, you gonna tell me what the fuck happened?" Brandon demanded, anger scarcely hiding his concern.

"I saved Karyn. It would have got her in the side

of the chest or the neck, right into her heart or lungs or jugular or something." He gazed at the coffee, at the swirling tendrils of steam reaching for him like fingers grasping at his face. To make it worse, the curling mist only served to remind him that he desperately wanted a cigarette right about now.

Brandon looked stunned. Then: "So…hang on. You discharged yourself?" What Julian was saying was only just slowly dawning on the weary journalist.

Julian shrugged just a little, as much as the pain would allow, then nodded.

Brandon looked at him curiously, then made his way cautiously behind his old friend. "Oh, for fuck's sake, Julian," he groaned. The blood stain was wet and fresh, soaking through the heavy bandages and two layers of clothing, and growing larger even as he watched. "You need to…"

"No, I…" he started, but then fell silent. His eyes rolled in their sockets, and he swayed slightly. After a few moments, he placed his palm on his forehead and rubbed it hard. "Shit," he finally murmured.

"You need to get back to the hospital. Now." Brandon grabbed a jacket and slid it on.

"Yeah, but…" He had to shake his head again. "I need your high school yearbooks," he stated quickly.

"My what?" Pants now, pulled over his pajama bottoms uncomfortably.

"The yearbooks. From high school." He stared at Brandon. "I think mine are at dad's place, who knows where, but I need them soon. The last two, years eleven and twelve." His eyes were clearly having trouble focusing.

"Why didn't you just ring me?" Brandon asked. "Why couldn't this wait until morning? Why this urgency?"

"Because I need to do this." Julian's mind was whirling; Brandon could see the confusion, but also the strange determination. Time was irrelevant; to him, this simply had to be done now. "And because you can't leave the house," he went on suddenly. "You can't leave your kids alone." He stood uneasily. "You've got more to lose than the rest of us, and you are now the only one left." Brandon couldn't help but notice that the bloodstain had left a mark on the back of the chair as well.

Then Julian's words struck him. "You believe me about this? It being against us?" He forced himself to look his old friend in the eyes. *The only one left.* The phrase tried to flash in the forefront of his mind like a warning beacon, but he could not bring himself to focus on that now.

In response to his question, Julian nodded once, slowly. "Brandon, I really need those books."

"Why?"

"Please, Brandon, I'll explain later when I feel…" His breath started to come in sharp, panting gasps. "I know you've got them; I don't know about the others. You're the one who's cared most about the past. You're the one who's kept tabs on us for all these years."

"Julian…"

"Books. Please." He paused as he carefully sat back down. "And then if you could call me a taxi. You're right.

I do need to get back. I feel like shit."

Brandon almost ran to his study. Julian had been correct—he knew exactly where everything was, and within moments he had both the thick yearbooks in his hands, as well as a towel to drape over Julian's shoulder.

But he could not help but check in on Kristina and Allan, asleep in their respective bedrooms.

The only one left.

"Please, God, no," he whispered and hurriedly returned to the other end of his house and his wounded friend.

1991

Francis fell back, sitting heavily on the grass, out of breath, staring at the girl lying before him, still half-encased in the plastic bag, her hands now unbound, tears streaming down his face.

Julian placed a hand on his shoulder, but he shrugged it off. "She was my friend," he whispered. "More than my friend. Why the fuck did we even think this was a good idea?"

"The ritual says it must be a loved one," Troy stated blandly, trying to reassert control over the situation. "And she was the closest thing to someone we all…"

"Fuck your ritual!" Francis screamed, leaping to his feet and then violently tackling Troy to the ground. "Fuck you! Fuck this power shit! She was my friend! You only chose her because your pathetic, petty jealousy couldn't let someone else be her friend!" He grabbed Troy by the collar and bounced his head off the ground. "I loved her! I really loved her! She was my best friend. My. Best. Friend." He accentuated those last words with three more head attacks on Troy.

"Come on, get off him!" Randolph growled, pulling back on Francis.

Francis let go of Troy and knocked Randolph's arms away. "You're just as bad!" he hissed. "I've seen the photos you've got of her. Don't tell me you don't fantasize about her as well." His lips curled into a cruel sneer. "When you found out we'd made love, you didn't talk to me for a fortnight. Think I didn't notice, you jealous prick?"

"Come on, man, that's not fair," Randolph whispered hoarsely, backing away.

"And you did agree to this as well," Julian stated coldly.

Francis glared at him but could not find any words to say. Julian was right, and even now Francis could not fathom what he had been thinking.

Especially this afternoon when they had made their final plans.

He turned away from them all as it finally hit him—completely, utterly, and wholly.

This was all his fault. Dear God, it was all on him.

Chapter Fifteen

2012

Julian just knew they'd be together, even at this ungodly hour of the morning, and so, after sweet-talking a nurse, including promising he would not leave again until they all thought he was ready, he was escorted to the room where Chantelle had already spent too much time.

Luke was there as well—apparently, some influence had been exerted to bend many hospital rules—and greeted him warmly; he didn't even acknowledge the sling or thickly bandaged shoulder as he led him across to the bed. "Julian, this is Chantelle," he beamed. The girl smiled weakly at him. She looked thin and pale and very ill, but she was awake and certainly looked more alive than the last time he had seen her. "Chantelle, this is another of those men I told you about, one of the Round Table—Julian, Doctor Julian Worthington."

"Round Table; that's something I haven't heard in years," Julian mused, smiling just a little.

"Dad told me about it a couple of days ago," piped up another voice. Julian looked over and saw Nathan on the other side of the bed in his wheelchair; influence was really bending the rules here. "But he wouldn't say why you all stopped hanging out." He smiled in such an innocent manner, but Julian could see the intelligence and genuine inquiry—and even the accusation—behind that gaze.

"Hey, I heard you were better," Julian said to Chantelle, avoiding Nathan's subtle probing, "and I'm glad you're somehow in here as well..." He nodded at the teenaged boy. "...so I can show both of you something, something I'm pretty sure neither of you would have seen before." He pulled the pair of yearbooks out of his sling and dropped them on the bed. "The height of the Round Table," he declared proudly, tapping the book from their final year of high school, "and the year before that, just because," he went on, touching the second.

"Dibs on the final one," Nathan smiled, snatching it quickly.

Chantelle grinned back at him and took the other. But within moments, they were comparing photographs of their respective parents, and then the other men they had met recently. Luke pointed out the members of the Round Table they hadn't yet come across, choking a little when he indicated Troy's pictures.

That was when Nathan started to look through the rest of the photos of the year twelve students; though black and white, each shot was a clear head-and-shoulders picture of each person, twelve to an A4 page, with a list of their achievements beneath. Some, like Randolph, simply had a list of their chosen subjects, while others, like Francis, had a long run-down of schooling achievements, club memberships, volunteer work, sports, and anything else the school felt was relevant.

Julian leaned forward a little. This was exactly what he had been waiting for. He just hoped it was all for naught. Because anything else was…

Nathan suddenly stopped, the smile on his face fading. "Can I…?" he sort of asked as he took the book from Chantelle's hands. He flicked through the photos of the members of their grade when they had been a year younger—just pictures with names and subjects, twenty to a page for the year elevens.

He finally found the image he was after and held it beside the larger one taken twelve months later. Chantelle carefully maneuvered herself to look at what he was staring at, then gasped loudly and covered her mouth, jerking the needle messily out of her elbow as she did so.

Julian was there before Luke even realized what was going on.

"What is it?" he asked, hoping he was keeping his absolute dread successfully in check.

Nathan pointed with some caution at one particular photograph. It stood out in stark contrast to all those surrounding it—the subject was the most beautiful girl in the book by far, her hair styled for the shot, hanging over one shoulder, so long its full length couldn't be ascertained, her visible breast clearly fully developed, her smile sweet, her eyes big and bright. In the other earlier picture, the smile and eyes were the same, the hair not as long, the physical development still growing, yet still the same person. Most definitely the same person, just shyer. The first image was not a trick; this girl was and apparently always had been just like this—gorgeous.

Julian struggled with his emotions but managed to keep them under control. "What about her?" he asked as casually as he could.

"She was the girl who interrupted my Skype session when I was hurt," Nathan muttered.

"Yeah?" Chantelle croaked. "That was the face I saw when that guy..." Tears started as too many memories suddenly flooded her mind, inundating her in a tsunami of negativity. "You know," she finished lamely, letting her father wrap his arm around her trembling shoulders as he tried to have a look as well, fearing the absolute worst.

"Are you sure?" Julian asked. "I mean, really sure?"

"How could you forget a face like that?" Nathan laughed, but there was no joy in the sound.

Julian glanced at Luke as he carefully moved the two books to give his old friend a better view. Luke peered uneasily at the pictures Nathan still indicated.

He swallowed hard, and on instinct, he held Chantelle closer to him in his sudden shock. "But...but that's impossible," he whispered.

Julian just returned his gaze to the image.

The photograph of Chelsea Hartog from more than twenty years before stared back at them with the sweetest of smiles on her innocent, beautiful, near-perfect face.

1991

To Francis's amazement, his former high school classmates who would not have given him the time of day before Christmas now, in January, at Chelsea's home, treated him as they did any other person at the party. He drank beer, shared jokes, and just talked. Only once, when a group laughed at his story of what had happened to the disliked Father O'Connor on one of the student retreats, did he wonder what the rest of the Round Table would think if they saw him right now. Suddenly accepting this invitation after avoiding two other post-exam gatherings was the best idea he'd had in years.

"Franky," whispered a voice in his ear, "can I see you?" He turned from the rest of the group listening to the former captain of the football team regale them all with his talks of personal heroism on the playing field and smiled at Chelsea.

"Sure," he replied, following her through the large house to the room where everyone had placed their birthday gifts for her. The pile was high beneath a handmade sign that read, "Happy 18th Chelsea!," which was decorated with photographs from the girl's life, showing more than anything else that she had always been physically attractive. "An adult," he smirked.

"Yeah, but my twenty-first will be better," she replied.

"Why?"

"Twenty-one is my lucky number," she said with the slightest of grins as she moved him into the room. She closed the door behind them, and Francis turned to face her, unsure of what was going on here. She looked at him for a brief moment and then grabbed his face with both hands and crushed her lips against his. For a few seconds, he just stood there, stunned, and then he dared to wrap his arms around her waist and draw her in closer. She came unhesitatingly into his embrace and shifted her hands to the back of his neck.

Mouths parted slightly. Eyes closed. Heads tilted. Tongues touched, lips pushed hard. For what seemed to Francis to be not nearly long enough, they kissed.

Francis felt the whole world disappear; all that existed was Chelsea; all that mattered was the two of them.

They parted reluctantly, and Francis could not stop grinning even as he caught his breath. "Uhh, what…?" he started, but could not let the words come out without sounding downright rude or, even worse, stupid.

She smiled oh so sweetly and kindly at him. "I told you I'd thank you properly for all you did for me," she whispered.

"Come on, I just gave you a hand with…"

"No," she interrupted firmly. "No. You—*you*—taught me how to study. You made sure I passed those history and math exams. You helped me with those bits of math and biology when the teachers couldn't be bothered. And you listened to me." Her face fell a little. "You probably know more about me than any of my friends out there." She kissed his cheek. "I just wish…" She let the comment hang in the air.

But Francis understood. This was it, one time, thank you, then continue their holiday break until university started, and from then on they'd "enjoy" a passing acquaintance. He reached across and risked kissing her again. She let it go for a few brief seconds before breaking it off; Francis did not fail to notice that she was still smiling. "I do owe you for something else, by the way," she breathed.

He looked at her with some confusion. She reached behind her and pulled a plain-wrapped gift from the pile, one Francis recognized straight away. "I snuck a look at most of them," she laughed. "And I reckon this one could well be my favorite."

Francis felt his smile return. "Really? Seriously?"

"I said you knew me better than any of my other friends," she said as a single tear—of joy? of sadness? He wasn't sure—ran down her cheek. He touched it, and she covered his hand with hers. "They gave me clothes and make-up and jewelry and videos and CDs and stuff like that." She held his gift up. "You treated me like an intelligent person. This shows you know what's important to me, where my head's at. You know me."

Francis took the three book set out of her hands and placed it back on the pile, then slowly approached her. She did not wait; she grabbed him again, and this time, there was more to the kiss than a mere thank you. He entwined his hands in her hair, and she responded in kind. She tasted a little like a wine cooler, but that didn't matter. He had hardly ever dared to dream this might happen, and yet here he was, living it...

The door closed suddenly, and they separated like two naughty children caught out. Chelsea giggled and let her forehead fall against Francis's. "Oops," she said, then recoiled a little.

She bent down and picked up an envelope from the floor. "Oops," she repeated with a giggle and tore it open. The card was very ornate, and she opened it, then removed a gift certificate for a day spa. She rolled her eyes. "Three of these and counting," she muttered, then, "Oh, listen to this: 'Your graceful legs are like jewels, the work of a craftsman's hands. Your navel is a rounded goblet that never lacks blended wine. Your waist is a mound of wheat encircled by lilies. Your breasts are like'—oh, Lord, really?—'like two fawns, twins of a gazelle.' Seriously?"

"It's from the Bible, *Song of Songs*," Francis said. "And, sorry, and no offense to whoever gave it to you—that's sad."

"Too right, it is."

"Look, can I ask who it's from?"

She read the bottom and shrugged. "It just says, 'TW.' I don't think I know a TW." She tossed it over her shoulder like yesterday's rubbish and rewrapped her arms around his neck. "Now, where were we?" Her kiss sent a fire through him, a feeling that was so wonderful and perfect he hoped it would never end.

A shiver ran through him.

Francis did know who it was who had thrown that card in here. And for a few fleeting moments, before he completely lost himself with this girl again, he wondered just what was going on with his old friend, and what he was even doing here, and how he would be after seeing the two of them together.

But then it was Chelsea. Chelsea was all that mattered. Chelsea was all that would ever matter…

Chapter Sixteen

2012

Brandon sat on an old wicker chair on the front porch of his house as his two eldest children played with a soft, round ball, trying to emulate the soccer game they'd just finished watching on television. And, like most five-year-olds, they simply did not stop. They had already asked Brandon countless times to join them, but after the previous night's nocturnal visitor, he felt was simply too tired to do it safely. What he really wanted was to catch up on some sleep, but Tara was with the younger two children at their pre-schoolers' swimming lesson, and so he was awake and here.

The phone in his pocket sounded loudly, its ring tone a recording of an old-fashioned dial-up phone, the volume enough to jar him out of a near-sleep. He pulled it out slowly and pressed it to his ear without checking the number. "Brandon Cornelius," he stated emotionlessly.

"Hey, mate, it's me, Julian." The tone of voice made him sit up immediately, spilling his coffee on his pant leg. "Look, I know this is weird, but just get your kids, the twins, and don't let them out of your sight for an instant. Now, Brandon; I'm serious."

"I can see them right now," he replied, running his hand over the wet patch. "Now, are you going to tell me what's wrong?"

"It's Chelsea."

That name was enough to send ice through Brandon's veins, freezing him into immobility, his eyes not seeing anything.

"C'mon, Krissie, kick it harder!" young Allan yelled at his twin sister. The girl obeyed with a loud squeal. The ball bounced off her brother's chest and onto the road.

Brandon hardly noticed. "Julian, Chelsea's dead," he said simply, rubbing his forehead with his hand. A headache had suddenly and uncomfortably decided to make itself known.

"You think I don't know that?" There was a pause while he calmed himself. "Look, I'm coming over. The nurses will kill me, but I need to tell you something that doesn't make any sense. As soon as I've seen Francis, I'll be there, okay? Just look out for my taxi." He sounded a touch embarrassed. "And I might need some help to pay for it. Luke's hidden my wallet."

"Are you going to tell me what's going on?" This was all impossible, and Brandon's voice felt distant to his own ears. He continued to stare at the spilled coffee as though that was the most important thing in the world.

He didn't see his two children standing at the edge of the road, looking left, then right, then left, then right, again and again, while the ball sat on top of a metal disc that covered some utility or another in the center of the bitumen.

Brandon lifted his face.

Holding hands, the twins ran out together.

Too late, Brandon's mind registered what was happening. He dropped the phone and stood, even though his legs were suddenly made of lead. "No…" he tried, but all that came out was a hoarse croak.

"Brandon! Brandon!" Julian's tinny voice was screaming out of the phone on the ground.

The car screeched around the corner.

Brandon opened his mouth to cry out, but the driver's face turned and gazed at him. In that briefest of moments, he was sure he could see who she was.

But it couldn't be…

The children merely stared at the oncoming vehicle in dumb fascination.

"Jump!" Brandon finally found his voice; his command was the only one that came to mind.

The twins obeyed automatically, Allan leaping to the left, Kristina to the right.

The car struck them both at the same time, crashing into their hips and sending them skidding off to opposite sides of the road, lifeless, like discarded ragdolls.

Neither moved.

The car lost control and plowed into a parked utility vehicle.

And Brandon fell to his knees, his eyes vague and unfixed, unable to see anything before him.

And wanting to never see anything else ever again.

1991

All of the others stared at Francis.

"Oh, I get it," Troy said coldly after a time. "You were going to stop us from doing this, and that would have made you into a hero. This strange relationship, this on–off thing you have with her would be on again, maybe even permanently. Right?"

"Don't be so fucking stupid," Francis growled, and yet his eyes dropped to once more gaze upon the body of the beauty before them.

"Look, we all liked her, most of us from afar—" Nearly all the rest averted their eyes at that. "—but you know what we want. We want the power and influence, and we want to be in control, like everything we had in that last year of high school, only more so. We want it for the rest of our lives. We want to dominate. What we want is almost impossible to attain. Only this—" He held the book up. "—can give us all that. The greatest of desires. That's what we are aiming for: our greatest of desires. And only through a loved one's sacrifice can the greatest of desires even hope to be delivered…"

"It's all bullshit!" Francis cried, cutting off Troy's speech. "I can't believe we even went along with this in the first place." He looked around at all the others, making sure of at least a moment of eye contact. "Are we that desperate that we've resorted to believing in fairy tales?"

"It worked!" Sean returned, suddenly and passionately. "Troy got money! I got..." He let his voice fade as he looked down, embarrassed.

"What?" Francis hissed. "You did this shit as well?"

"I borrowed the book," he mumbled sheepishly. "Did it on my own." He finally looked at the rest. "Troy was the only one who knew. I made him swear to keep it secret."

Everyone stared at him in surprise except Troy, who was nodding sagely. "Go on, tell them," he insisted, everything about his manner that of a man who'd won the most important argument of his life.

Sean groaned and wiped his eyes. "Remember how they said Teresa was going to die, but she pulled through, like some sort of a miracle?" he whispered. "And remember how our dog Trixie died at the same time? Our beloved dog?" He cast his eyes around and nodded, as if that explained everything.

"Oh, for fuck's sake," Francis growled. Of course, they remembered; Teresa, Sean's older sister, had been a passenger in a car that had slammed into a tree in the early hours of New Year's Day. Her chances of survival had been minimal, and even if she did come out of it, the family had been told that the brain damage would be profound. To everyone's surprise, including the doctors, she had made a sudden and complete recovery, with only the scars showing through the hair that was still regrowing giving any indication that it had ever taken place. The family put it down to the power of prayer; the doctors to a poor prognosis on their behalf. But to Francis, something else concerned him. "You killed Trixie?" he finally asked, but that went ignored by his friends in the stunned shock.

"You never said," Luke muttered.

"Oh, but I knew," Troy gloated. "Sure, with me, it could have been a coincidence. But not this, not Teresa."

"I wish I'd known," Francis mumbled, reaching across to stroke the long, golden locks of the girl in the bag.

"Why?" Troy sneered.

"Because I would have known just how fucking serious you were about this crap," he stated angrily, "and I would *never* have agreed to even contemplate this bullshit."

Chapter Seventeen

2012

"It must be over now," Sean whispered.

The four men with him did not even move. Finally: "How do you work that one out?" Francis asked.

"Logic," he stated with strange detachment. "All of us have had our eldest kids taken—or tried to be taken—from us. Chelsea was the eldest. Whoever's doing this has got what they wanted, clearly. So, that's got to be it." He struggled to keep himself from crying. "Some of us lost our children, others were really lucky…" He seemed to be fighting an internal battle not to cast an accusing eye at Julian. "…but it's got to be over now. Doesn't it?"

It took a while before anyone dared to formulate an answer.

"I don't know, but…" Francis stopped as the intercom buzzed and some garbled, distorted voice announced that a car was parked illegally. Francis found himself looking at his watch. He should have been in court half an hour ago with one of his firm's more valuable clients; he only hoped his junior barrister was doing a good enough job to keep the old man happy. He snapped back to reality; his mind was wandering to keep itself from thinking about the maelstrom swirling about him. He resumed, feeling the others' eyes on him. "…but, shit, I hope it is."

Randolph stood, his face a barely contained volcano, and started out of the waiting room.

"What's up, mate?" Luke asked.

"Can't do this," he mumbled from between clenched teeth. "Can't." Luke went to stand up to follow, but Sean placed a firm hand on his shoulder and shook his head. Luke saw it in Sean's eyes, and then he understood not only the reasoning but also the emotion behind Sean's actions. Luke could not really comprehend what was going through Sean's mind; Chantelle was in a bed upstairs with Nathan probably right beside her. He had not gone through the ultimate loss.

At that simple thought of his daughter, he gazed upward, in the direction of her room, only vaguely aware that Sean had now taken off after Randolph.

Yes, despite everything, Luke had apparently somehow managed to get "lucky," thank God.

***

Unaware of—and not overly concerned with—her father's proximity, Chantelle was lying on her back, eyes closed, listening to Nathan read the book he had started before she had even known him, a slight smile on her face.

Gradually, and ever so subtly, her hand reached along the bed and came to rest on his forearm. Her fingers wrapped around his muscular limb tightly. He missed a beat in his reading, and when he managed to resume, it was with the slightest hint of a grin on his lips.

"Time for a quick obs." The voice of a nurse interrupted Nathan's story-telling, and Chantelle's hand darted back to her hip as the red flush of embarrassment colored her cheeks.

"S'pose it's time for me to get going then," Nathan said with a slightly exaggerated sigh, gripping the wheels of his chair.

"No." Chantelle's hand returned to his arm. "Stay. Please."

He offered her a nervous smile and cocked his head to one side. "If you really want." There was more hope in his voice than he was entirely comfortable with.

"It's your call," the nurse stated without hesitation or judgment.

"I do." Chantelle's response was immediate, and her eyes did not leave Nathan's.

The nurse offered a very slight shrug and carefully pulled back the sheets and blankets. "You sure?" she asked once more; Chantelle merely nodded. The nurse lifted the hospital gown, revealing a pair of lycra running shorts and a stomach completely swathed in bandages. Some rust-colored stains showed through on the edges, and the nurse grunted. "I'll come back to change those dressings later," she said with disinterest. Again, Chantelle just nodded. The nurse then pressed down on top of where the surgeon's incision was. Chantelle winced and gripped Nathan's forearm. The older woman moved her fingers outwards with expert precision, and Chantelle's wincing diminished. The nurse then grabbed a clipboard. "You eat anything today?" she asked mechanically.

"Uhh, I had water for breakfast, but I had some soup for lunch."

"Any feelings of nausea afterward?"

Chantelle shook her head.

"Well, I think you've got sandwiches and tea tonight, so see how you with that." The nurse cast Nathan a quick sideways glance. "Bowel movements?"

"Uhh, no, not yet," was the soft response, "but I walked to the toilet this morning for, erm, number ones."

"Okay." She looked at the chart. "It's not noted here. Do you remember who took you?"

Chantelle looked at Nathan. "Red-haired nurse. Young-ish," she said, unsure of herself.

"They took a drip on a stand with them," Nathan added. "I reckon it must've been ten-thirty or so."

The nurse sighed again and made a note. She then placed everything back where it had been and stared at Chantelle, her eyes a touch more vacant than before. "Time for a painkiller, then," she stated with no emotion in her voice at all.

"What about pulse rate, blood pressure, and the other stuff?" Chantelle asked, the first touch of worry clouding her question.

The nurse gave no indication she had even heard.

She simply pulled a syringe out of her top pocket and then unwrapped a fresh needle, which she attached carefully. She pulled back the plunger, filling the plastic tube with nothing but air, and then gripped it in a tight fist.

She looked up at the two teenagers.

The middle-aged woman was not the person staring at them. The face was suddenly so much younger and stunningly beautiful, framed by long, golden hair that shone in the harsh fluorescent lighting. It was a face they recognized immediately, and which sent a chilled dagger into both of their hearts. Chantelle gasped and closed her eyes; Nathan could only watch. The nurse's thumb was poised over the plunger. One final gorgeous smile and then she stabbed it down hard and fast.

The needle stuck, and she forced her thumb onwards.

It didn't depress.

Her beautiful eyes darted downwards, showing anger and confusion for the first time. But when the face gazed back at them, the older nurse's visage had returned, and the expression on her face could only be described as one of absolute horror. She stumbled backward, knocking a vase from the side table, her mouth agape, tears filling her eyes, then turned and fled.

The two youngsters watched her go, wide-eyed, Nathan's body tense, Chantelle's shaking violently, the stain on her bandage growing worryingly.

Then they slowly lowered their eyes to the book Nathan had thrust painfully onto Chantelle's stomach.

To the book and the hypodermic syringe quivering

from the front cover like a well-aimed, deadly dart.

Chantelle burst into pained, wracking sobs and reached for Nathan automatically. He hugged her close to him. She held him so tight he struggled to move, but he forced himself to, at least enough to grab his mobile phone from the bag attached to his wheelchair. He held Chantelle for a few moments, his hand on the back of her head, her face buried in his neck, then typed a simple message to his father:

"Come here now."

1991

The first round of university offers arrived in the mail; the previously organized celebratory party was at Francis's house, in the rumpus room—formerly a two-car garage—out back. Just them in the room with alcohol and food, and Francis's parents simply letting them go; in all the years of this friendship, nothing untoward had ever happened, so why would it start now?

As had become their custom, they all arrived within five minutes of one another, except Troy, who was his usual twenty minutes late. They found it hard to keep a lid on things until he arrived, even though to Francis's mind it was all strangely subdued, even somber, and yet they drank beer around the large table, which had hosted years of games of *Dungeons & Dragons*, *Risk*, *Trivial Pursuit*, and dozens of others, and just waited.

Troy's eventual arrival heralded the beginning of a ritual they had decided upon half-way through their final year of high school. But Francis could already feel it was not right. Still, the show must go on, he told himself.

It was Francis who stood first. "Gentlemen, pre-law," he said with pride.

"Huzzah!" the others responded before they all swallowed a mouthful of beer.

Julian next. "Didn't get into engineering, but I'm happy enough with science. If I don't get in on the second round, maybe I'll transfer across if I get good enough marks in first year."

"Huzzah!" Swallow, done immediately, to hide curious glances. Julian didn't get his first choice?

Luke stood, a little self-consciously. "I made it. Physiotherapy."

That was better. "Huzzah!" Another drink.

A pause, then Sean stood next, almost reluctantly. "Accounting, but I'll try for an accounting-economics double degree when I go in for orientation week."

"Huzzah." But it was nowhere near as hearty a cheer. That hadn't been Sean's first choice—not even his second—and they all knew it. And he was not even considering getting a better offer in the second round.

Another longer pause before Brandon pushed himself slowly to his feet. "Journalism." His voice was quiet, ashamed, his eyes downcast.

"Huzzah." It was intoned, with not even a touch of emotion.

"Yeah, huzzah," Brandon echoed as he sat heavily.

"But I, I mean, we, but we thought you wanted to write and..." Francis blustered.

"Journalism was my second option," Brandon muttered. "Pre-law was what I wanted, but my grades…" He looked at Francis. "Really wanted," he added grimly.

Randolph then stood. "That's what I wanted as well," he stated but then fell silent.

"Well?" Julian urged.

"My last choice, the one grandpa wanted me to do." He sneered then as he spat, "Accounting."

"At least I won't be alone," Sean muttered.

"Huzzah." This clearly was not going the way they had planned or hoped at all.

Troy was last. He looked at all of them with a smile on his face. "I got the one all private school students get offered if they actually pass their final year, and I only just passed: Liberal Arts. I guess I'll see what subjects I can pick, then see what sort of dead-end job I can get at the end of it all." He held up his bottle. "Huz-fucking-zah."

No-one bothered to respond. He had refused to tell anyone his results, so they knew it had been bad, but now they knew he at least hadn't failed. Still, how could the Round Table have fallen so hard?

Then:

"English Literature." They all turned suddenly, and Francis almost jumped to his feet.

"Chelsea!" he cried. "What brings you here?" His broad smile grew even wider as she grabbed him tight and kissed him loudly.

"I did it!" she squealed happily. "I made it into uni, what I wanted, and it's all because of you!" She then looked around the table at the others, keeping a firm hold on Francis's hand. "So, I guess we'll all be at the same school again.

"Huzzah!" Troy said with a partially forced smile.

"Huzzah!" the others echoed, and the tone of the gathering changed markedly. False fronts were plastered onto each of them, trying to make this seem like a celebration and not the wake it had threatened to become. Glories of the future—what university might bring, what could happen beyond formal education—were not what they focused on; instead, talk drifted to high school reminiscences, of times when they had influence and success. They did not let a hint of their concern about the sudden and dramatic lack of power they all felt, especially with so many of them not living up to their personal expectations show; not the fact their lives were no longer in their control; not even that sudden feeling of helplessness—even within those who had achieved what they wanted thus far—sat incredibly uneasily on them all. They were about to go from the top of one of the best schools to bare beginners in a tertiary institution, many having, in their eyes, failed already. This terrified them.

And all Chelsea's presence did was keep that fear bottled up and festering...

Chapter Eighteen

2012

"Dad, are you going to tell me what the fuck is going on?" Nathan demanded.

Francis just continued to drive, his hands clenching the steering wheel so tight his knuckles were white, not even telling his son off for swearing.

Nathan shook his head and stared out the window, watching the cityscape slowly turn into suburbia. "This isn't the way home," he stated through a tight jaw. "You at least going to tell me where you're taking me?"

Francis did not relax. "Yeah, you're staying at the Archer place for a few days."

"What?" Nathan shook his head. "What about school? What about my friends? It's bad enough I can't play football, and you're all paranoid about everyone who's not one of your old mates, but I'm the school Captain, and I've already missed too much class time, and exams are..."

"I know, I know!" Francis yelled suddenly, slapping his palms against the top of the wheel, jerking the car sideways. "I know," he repeated, "but we just want to keep all you kids together, just until we can work out what's going on." He paused briefly, debating with himself what he should say next, and decided that anything but honesty was going to catch him out. "The others really want you there. The way you've helped Chantelle, especially keeping your cool when that nurse... Look, you're probably the most 'with it' of the lot of them, and they all trust you."

"But Chantelle's older. She's already at uni, and I'm just..."

"Chantelle wants you there as well," Francis said quietly. "She's scared, mate, really scared."

Nathan fell silent again. He didn't have an answer to that; he could not let Chantelle down. His body tensed up. Where had that thought come from? Yet, he had to admit, the idea of spending more time with Chantelle was quite pleasant. "So, me and Chantelle," he mused.

"And Karyn Worthington and Allan Cornelius." Francis turned a corner carefully. "You need to keep a good eye on Allan. He's in a bad way. They're still not sure if Kristina's going to pull through."

"So, why isn't he still in the hospital?" Nathan couldn't help but ask. "Didn't he shatter his pelvis or something?"

"Broken, cracked, yeah, and he's all bandaged. They decided against a full cast. But, seriously, after what happened to Chantelle..." He let his voice drift off. "Nath,

I'm really proud of you," he said, his voice cracking a little. "You didn't panic…" The younger man opened his mouth to protest. "Chantelle said you didn't panic," Francis corrected. "You just did what had to be done." He swallowed a sour, heavy lump rising in his throat. "I just wish I'd been like that when I was your age." He struggled to keep his emotions in check. "Then maybe none of this would be happening."

"So, what's going on, dad? Tell me, please," Nathan begged suddenly, exasperation evident in his tone.

"I wish I could." Francis sniffed back the tears that had finally broken free. "I really wish I could…"

1991

Francis could not bring himself to stand up.

Chelsea was lying still in front of him, and all his friends were staring at him, and all he felt like doing was crawling into the earth and disappearing.

This was not something he had ever, ever imagined facing. His future, everything he had worked so hard to achieve in his life, everything his family had wanted for him, it was all as dead as the girl before him.

He finally risked casting a glance at his comrades. None could return his glare. None except Troy.

The absolute fury on his face was unconcealed.

Francis's own anger rose in response. "We've killed her," he hissed.

"And all for nothing," Troy returned evenly.

"What? Is that all you've got to say? It was for nothing? What does that even fucking mean? She's real, a person, not a…a…" He struggled for the right word, but it didn't come. "…a fucking thing!"

"You don't understand." Troy's demeanor remained gruff and full of bile.

"No. No, I fuckin don't." He stroked the girl's forehead, the skin cold and clammy. "Why did I…"

"HNUUH!"

Chelsea's eyes shot open, and she inhaled a deep, throaty breath. She swallowed hard and tried to sit up but instead collapsed onto her back again, panting heavily.

The worried expressions on the teenaged boys around her actually grew a little more concerned.

Troy pulled out the book once more and surreptitiously opened it to a pre-marked page.

But all the others could do was continue to stare with a mixture of relief and sheer, absolute terror.

Chapter Nineteen

2012

Nathan was finding it rather difficult to concentrate as he typed the name into Google on the unfamiliar PC. Chantelle was sitting beside him, somehow sharing his chair while still sitting on her own, her head resting on his shoulder, her hair hanging down across the top of his chest, her hand gently cradling her aching stomach. He could feel her breath as a pleasant zephyr against his cheek and struggled to control his body, especially when her other hand came to rest on his upper thigh.

The search results flashed up, diverting his attention. Almost a million hits. He wouldn't have thought "Chelsea Hartog" was that common a name.

He took note of the very first one and started. It was a link to a Facebook page titled "20 Years Ago— Remembering Chelsea Hartog." He clicked on it, and both of them read the opening spiel: "20 years ago, on September 16ᵗʰ, 1991, my older sister Chelsea disappeared. No trace of her has ever been found. If you remember & still love Chelsea, please share this page." Almost a year had passed since the page had been created, they noted, but with over fifteen thousand "likes" and the latest comment coming only two days earlier, it was certainly not a dead page.

On a whim, Nathan scrolled down the comments section, right to the bottom of the history, then slowly worked his way up. It took about five minutes, but he found what he had been sure—and yet fearful—that he would find: "September 16, 2011, 11:56 p.m: Francis Coulter. Still in our hearts. I'll never forget her. ☹" This was followed by an indication of sixty-three "likes" of what had been typed.

The comment underneath, in response, was also telling: "September 17, 2011, 6:14 a.m.: Jasmine Desiderato. She really liked you, Franky. You were so good for her." Twelve "likes."

There were several other comments about the apparent strong relationship that had existed between this missing girl and his father, then Chantelle stopped his hand. "That's dad," she stated, pointing at the screen.

"Luke Bowman?"

"He's a teacher, remember?" she explained. "He doesn't want any of his students to find him, troll him. Get him into trouble, whatever. So, you know—Archer, Bowman." She laughed, a musical sound that tingled pleasantly down Nathan's spine. "He thinks it's clever."

"Parents, huh?" Nathan rolled his eyes, and this time, they both laughed and pressed their cheeks together. They parted slowly, in silence, and looked at one another, neither really smiling, their eyes fixed on the other's.

Chantelle bridged the gap with the lightest of kisses on his mouth with her amazingly soft lips. When she drew back, her grin was wide but coy, and she settled her hand once more on his leg. It took him a few seconds to compose himself before he could even begin to refocus on the computer monitor. He found himself wondering at her timing more than the emotion behind the kiss and decided that it was most likely a coping mechanism. He found that thought actually a little upsetting; he guessed a part of him wanted to believe it was more than that.

He shook his head clear; now was definitely not the time.

He read on:

"September 19, 2011, 8:01 p.m.: Luke Bowman. She was the best, mate. I just wish things could have worked out differently."

"September 19, 2011, 9:41 p.m.: Jasmine Desiderato. Here here!"

"September 19, 2011, 11:12 p.m.: Sophia Cuccitone. agree!"

"Wow," Chantelle murmured. "This looks like she and your dad really had something special."

"It does, doesn't it." Nathan suddenly felt he was prying into areas he shouldn't, but he couldn't help himself and could not stop.

"Does it actually say what happened?" Chantelle asked, placing her hand over his on the mouse and closing the page down to once more bring up the Google search results. She quickly scrolled down, then went to the second page. "There," she said.

Nathan nodded and opened up the year-old archived news article. **"20 Years Later and Still No Closure for the Hartog Family,"** the headline read. The article featured a picture of a woman who looked very old, a man who could have been a contemporary of their fathers and who it took Nathan a few moments to realize was a teacher from his school, and an image they immediately recognized from the final year high school yearbook they had been shown. Both skimmed the article, then sat back, Chantelle pulling away so she could see Nathan's face.

"Disappeared without a trace?" she whispered.

"That's what it says." Nathan looked at the screen again. "Last seen walking through a park on her way home from university, no sign of her since." He went back to Google and clicked on the next news-looking link, this one from 2008. "Holy shit," he whispered.

"What?" Chantelle was right against him again, but even the smell of her hair and feel of her skin did nothing for him as he highlighted a paragraph halfway down with the cursor. Chantelle read it out loud: ""The last persons known to have seen her alive were her close friend Francis Coulter and a classmate, Troy Washington. Even though Coulter admitted Washington and Chelsea argued, they were never seen as potential suspects according to police records.' Your dad was one of the last ones to see her alive?"

"So it would seem." Nathan closed his eyes and controlled his breathing until Chantelle rested her hand over his, entwined their fingers. "You don't think dad was involved, do you?" he asked, his emotions bubbling so very close to the surface.

"But she isn't missing, is she?" Chantelle looked at the photo on the screen, that gorgeous eighteen-year-old from so long ago. "I mean, we've seen her, haven't we?"

"Yeah, we sure have." They stared at one another. That *was* true… they supposed. Wasn't it?

Wasn't it?

Nathan shook his head. Chantelle took both his hands. They did not understand what all of this meant. It went against everything they both accepted as reality, but…

But it was there. Right there. Staring at them from a computer screen.

What in the hell was going on?

1991

Francis walked into the half-full university tavern, bought a beer, downed most of it, and then joined the other members of the so-called Round Table in a corner booth. He sat heavily and looked around. "Where's Luke and Randolph?" he asked.

"Randolph failed an essay and has until six this evening to resubmit," Sean said.

"And Luke's been shifted to a different tute group, so he won't be here for another half hour or so," Julian added, leaning back, hands behind his head. He snorted a laugh with barely a touch of humor. "Uni's pretty different from high school, isn't it?" he sighed wistfully and sadly.

"Different? Different? It's like two completely opposite worlds," Troy sneered. "I mean, they would never just change our classes in high school like that."

"And since when did any of us ever fail anything?" Brandon growled. Troy looked away at that. "Hell, I got a low pass on my first writing assignment. Me!"

"Maybe high school didn't really prepare us," Francis suggested, biting his tongue so he wouldn't make a comment about how few of them had achieved their first-choice university preferences. They had made assumptions, hadn't worked like they should have. And now he was judging his friends…

"Or maybe we don't have enough power and influence here to help us through comfortably," Troy snarled.

Francis groaned. "Come on, how is power and influence…" He made air quotes with his fingers over those three words. "…going to help us here? Hundreds and hundreds of students are here, and it looks to me like the only ones with any sort of power at all are the ones doing a Ph.D. or something like that." He shook his head and suppressed a wry smile. "That's just crappy high school shit that got us through high school by making sure we were left alone. Our test results, my Dux, they mean nothing. This is closer to real life. We have no real power or influence. Nothing. No under-grad does. No teenager does. No *kid* does…"

"That annoying shit Jefferson Mulkahy does," Brandon growled.

"Who?" Francis returned, the mind-numbing lecture he had just left fading into the background when faced with his complaining companions. His issues were minor; he almost laughed at himself for overreacting to one lousy, complex class.

"A little shit doing journalism. You know, the full course, not a couple of subjects." Brandon rammed his beer into his mouth messily. "Transferred from arts after one week, got put into the tutes and stuff of his choice, got help with the first assignments, everything."

"How'd he manage that?" Troy demanded.

"Father is a professor or something in the med school," Brandon growled. "At least, that's what some of the other guys say."

"So, surely there must be a way for people like us to get some sort of influence here as well," Sean mused.

"Why?" Francis sighed.

"We were the top students at one of the best schools in the state," Sean said incredulously, as though it was obvious.

Francis again struggled to not mention the fact that most of them had bombed out in their exams and had not even featured in the top lists at the end of the year. They were really looking at things with a distorted self-view. He finally forced himself to mutter, "Yeah. So?"

"What?" Troy's tone held anger and confusion, with distinctly more anger.

"Why do we need influence?" Francis asked. "We are smart enough. All we need is to work hard and we'll end up where we want to be. It's that simple. A few years here being the plebs will probably do us a world of good."

The rest fell silent, knowing he was absolutely correct, but none willing to admit it out loud, all of them missing the freedom and sort of power they felt they had been afforded in high school.

"Can I join you guys?"

They all looked up to be greeted by the beaming face of Chelsea. Francis slid across the seat a little so she could squeeze in beside him, draping one of her legs over his with casual abandon; his physical response was instantaneous, and she knew it. She placed a beer in front of him and her favorite gin and lemonade in front of herself. "Hi," he said, unable to hide his broad smile.

"Hi, yourself," she returned seductively and kissed him on the cheek.

"You seem to be in a particularly good mood." He smiled wider; the good mood was infectious, at least onto him.

"I am." She sipped her drink and stared at him through the tops of her eyes.

"Well?"

"Remember that essay you helped me with, the one on the Brontë sisters?"

"Sure, but you did most of the..."

She shook her head so vigorously her long ponytail whipped across his shoulders, settling there like a golden scarf. "No," she stated firmly. "I could never have done it without you, not like I did."

The others exchanged curious glances, feeling uncomfortable and excluded, but unwilling to move.

"Okay. Fine," Francis said with an exaggerated sigh. "What about it?"

"High distinction," she squealed and kissed him again. He slid his arm around her waist, and she let him pull her in closer.

"Well done," he enthused with a broad, dopey grin on his wide-eyed face. A few of the rest muttered their congratulations as well, but the two of them were lost in a private world of their own. They clinked their drinks together and giggled like school children as they drank. Now some of the others did turn away with discomfort; Troy's expression, however, was more intense, and his gaze remained fixed on his friend.

Then Francis asked, "Hang on. You've got a lecture this afternoon, haven't you?"

"Oh, I managed to get my timetables changed," she cooed. "So I've got, now, Friday afternoons off and every second Wednesday as well."

"How'd you manage that?" Sean asked suddenly.

She shrugged. "I just asked nicely and got what I wanted," she said. Then she returned her attention to Francis. "So, I've got the rest of this glorious day to myself." She raised her eyebrows. "I know you do, too. Want to do something?"

"You get the good grades, you get to choose."

She giggled again and kissed him on the cheek noisily.

"Oh, get a room," Troy growled.

Chelsea cast him a curious sideways glance. "Okay, fine," she stated, finishing her drink as she stood. She took Francis by the hand and dragged him to his feet. "Let's go," she said, her glare at Troy dismissive.

"I thought we were going to your place tonight for a few rounds of *Risk*," Brandon whined.

"Well…" Francis started uneasily. "Maybe later."

"Really?" Chelsea purred, wrapping around his arm like a happy snake.

"Sorry, guys. Some other time," Francis muttered dreamily.

"Yeah, sorry," Chelsea added. "Let's go, Franky!"

He obeyed wordlessly, like an abandoned puppy with a new owner.

"Nice," Brandon muttered.

"Yeah," Troy grumbled. "New friend, new…"

"No, you," Brandon interrupted.

"What? Me?" he was indignant and angrier.

"Yeah," Sean added. "She's got influence here as well. More influence than us. Hell, she's got influence *over* us."

"Well, over one of us, at least," Troy said coldly.

"Bullshit. If she asked you to get her a cup of coffee, you'd fly all the way to Brazil to make sure she had the best beans ever," Julian laughed, the rest joining in quickly.

"But," Sean went on suddenly, "if she's got so much

influence, why can't we have it as well?"

"Because none of us look like a super-model," Julian said, standing and throwing his chest out ridiculously. "Reckon I could pull it off?" The others all burst out laughing—even Troy—but the seed had once more been sown: the power and influence were out there and available. They just had to find a way to take it.

Chapter Twenty

2012

Francis disconnected the phone and stared at it for a long time, then cast a glance at Luke, who was still listening to a person on the other end of his device, before turning his attention to his son, sitting on the couch beside Chantelle. Their bodies leaned in to each other, her hand on his wounded thigh, their faces impassive.

He stared back at the phone until Luke had finished, unable to look their children in the eyes. Finally, Luke dropped his hands to his lap. "I guess you got the same message I did," he muttered,

"Little Kristina," Francis acknowledged, nodding once. "Yeah."

Chantelle's eyes widened. 'That little girl?" she whispered. "Is she…?"

Luke's forlorn expression was all the response she needed. She sobbed once, loudly, and then buried her face in Nathan's chest. He instinctively and immediately placed an arm around her. She pressed herself against him and his hand twisted in her hair, holding her tight. Luke, already starting to lift himself to comfort her, jolted visibly at the response. He dropped back down in his seat, unable to take his eyes from his daughter. Not what he had expected, not what he wanted, but also clearly not the time to comment.

"How's Brandon?" Nathan asked carefully.

Francis held his phone up as if that explained everything. "Shattered," he muttered.

Luke nodded. "Julian's with him. They've got Karyn and Allan with them as well." He tried to smile. "I guess they're not coming over after all."

The humor was lost on Nathan. "So, now what? We just wait for this woman to try again?" he demanded.

"Well, I don't think she can..." Francis began, but he could finish. "What can we do?" he tried.

"First, I think you better tell us what happened." Nathan glared at his father angrily, and the older man winced. Chantelle sat up but kept her hand on Nathan's leg, now staring at her own father with an intensity that made him more uncomfortable than he'd felt in years.

Luke and Francis glanced warily at one another. "Well, let's see," Luke said. "Chelsea was a girl from high school..."

"Dad," Chantelle said evenly, her eyes burrowing right into him, "we're not stupid."

"What do you mean?" he returned, again darting his eyes in Francis's direction.

Nathan took a deep breath, slowly and loudly exhaling from between his teeth. "We know she was dad's girlfriend, and she went to uni and high school with you," he explained. "You were really in love with her, you were one of the last people to see her alive, you…"

"Okay, enough," Francis said, barely keeping himself from yelling to stop his son. He could not help but once more gaze at Luke. "Enough," he repeated, calming himself.

"Yeah," Luke mumbled. "We ended up with two smart-arse kids, didn't we?"

"Ha, ha," Nathan said coldly. "So, what happened to Chelsea?" He glanced quickly at Chantelle, who nodded her encouragement and squeezed his hand. "Now, no bullshit. Something happened to her twenty-one years ago, in 1991, September, and I think you lot had something to do with it."

The two older men looked suddenly uncomfortable. "No," Francis said weakly, dropping his eyes.

"No?" Nathan mocked.

"No," he repeated softly, pathetically.

"Dad, stop the bullshit." Nathan wrapped his arm around Chelsea, almost protectively, and she fell eagerly into his embrace. "Whatever the fuck you lot did at university, it's affecting us, your kids. And I'm guessing after what happened to Chantelle in the hospital, this ain't stopping until we are dead. Dead. Us kids, the children of your fucking Round Table bullshit." Nathan's face was red when he finished, and all Francis could do was stare at him, and all he could think about was what the priests at his high school would think if they could hear their school Captain use language like that towards his own father.

Even if Francis believed that he deserved it.

"I... I... Look, I can't," Francis mumbled, surprised that tears were threatening to burst forth from his tired, itching eyes.

Nathan stood up slowly. Chantelle's hand kept hold of his briefly before dropping to the couch beside her, waiting for him to return. He limped across the room, gritting his teeth through the pain, physical and mental. He stopped and towered above the man who he had looked up to, virtually worshipped, for his whole life, more than any other person he had even heard of. But his expression turned harder and colder and he glowered through narrow eyes. "What did you do to her?" he rumbled, his anger a physical force pushing down on Francis.

"We... She disappeared," he offered weakly.

Nathan threw his head back in exasperation. "You're going to keep your pathetic secret, aren't you?" he hissed. "You care that little about us? Really? It doesn't matter that this woman is going to keep on coming after us until we are all dead. You're just..."

"But it can't be Chelsea!" Francis finally exploded. "It's impossible! You have to be wrong!"

"Why, dad? Go on. Tell me why."

Francis steeled himself for what he knew was coming. "Because Chelsea Hartog did not just disappear," he growled. "She is dead, dead and buried, and has been since 1991."

1991

"Franky, what are you doing?" Francis was at Chelsea's side quickly. "What's going on?"

"This was a…a joke, one that just got way too far out of hand," he whispered, hoping that what he was saying was going to be enough but knowing deep down that it wasn't. "I am so sorry. So very sorry. I didn't mean for it to get this far. I…"

"This far? This far? This far?!" Her hysteria was rising rapidly. "I'm kidnapped, drugged, tied up, thrown in a bag for how long? Three days? Longer? Then I'm dragged out here into the middle of nowhere by the guy I really, really like and his stupid, fucking, loser high school friends, and you tell me that this is all a joke and that it might have gone a bit far?" She shook her head. "You are such a fucking moron! Why are you…you of all people…doing this to me?"

"I don't know…" The first tears, the first of too many that would come over too many years, started.

She paused as she took them all in, each one of them. "I can see it. You think I'm going to let this pass, don't you?" she hissed. "Well, you think any of you are even going to be allowed to finish uni after I tell everyone what you've done to me? Three days in a bag except when that Washington pervert made me dress in this! Three days! I'm hungry, I'm cold, I've even fuckin' wet myself like a little kid! All of you, your lives are fucked! You hear me? You are all completely fucked!"

"Come on, Chelsea," Francis begged. "We'll get you home. We'll give you money. We'll do anything…"

"And so much for power and influence," Sean muttered.

"What? What the fuck does that even mean?" Chelsea now rounded on him. "What does any of this even mean? Can you tell me? Can you?"

Sean merely cowered visibly.

She spun and faced Troy next, the book still held open in front of him. "And what the fuck are you mumbling about over there? You. Yes, you. The one who raped me. Oh, yeah, raped me. Did you know that, Franky? Your mate here got me drunk, and I think he drugged me and had his way with me. Yep, that's right. That's what I was talking about in the caf' last time we were there. I wanted him to admit it, but the gutless prick wouldn't. That stupid shit fuckin' raped me!"

Francis glared at Troy. He tried to speak, but the words wouldn't come out. He understood now where all of this was coming from. And yet Troy ignored them both and continued with his reading.

"Yeah, you are all going down." She reached into the bag and struggled against the bonds still wrapped around her legs. "All of you!" It became a manic chant. "All of you! All of you!"

Troy suddenly slammed the book shut, threw his arms out and his head back, and then cried to the heavens, "And what we desire most of all is power and influence and the ability to change the world!"

His knife was then in his hands, as if out of nowhere.

"Oh, God," Francis whispered, still not wholly comprehending all that was occurring, but so very sure of what was about to happen before his very eyes. "No. Dear God, no…"

Chapter Twenty-One

2012

Nathan stared at his father for a long time. When the words came out, they were a confused jumble, a mirror of his stricken mind. "You… No… I… No… I can't…"

He turned his back on the older man to look at Chantelle, now lying on the couch in the fetal position, weeping softly. She was suddenly no longer an intelligent nineteen-year-old university student; she was an innocent child whose faith in all she had known and believed had just been shattered so completely it was as though her world had crumbled all around her.

"Look, we…" Francis started to say, but he knew no words would suffice. Not now. Maybe not ever. It had been there in Nathan's eyes before he had chosen to concentrate on the crying girl. It went beyond mere disappointment. It went beyond anger or sadness. It went beyond anything Francis had ever seen before.

Francis had lost his son.

An old saying suddenly hit him: The truth will set you free.

Well, this was not the freedom he wanted, set adrift from his own family.

Francis now let his vision drift to Luke. His old friend cringed in his chair as if expecting a physical blow. The truth hadn't really set him free, either.

The two fathers' eyes met. That simple action was too much for them. That night came back to them yet again, the images so stark and clear. Both abruptly returned their attention to their children.

Nathan squatted down in front of Chelsea, despite the pain in his leg. "Are you all right?" he asked so incredibly tenderly that Francis almost broke down. In the face of all this, his son was still a man. Something he could no longer say of himself.

She looked at him, her face flushed, her eyes red, her cheeks saturated. She shook her head slowly, then the sobs struck her again, jerking through her whole body. Nathan wrapped his arms tightly around her and held her close to him, and she returned the gesture, trying to hide against his body. Her arms did not want to let him go, and she cried against him as he stroked her hair and kissed the top of her head. They looked like they were the last two people left on Earth.

His next kiss was on her sweat-drenched forehead. "You feeling any better?" he asked.

She looked up at him and shook her head once more.

"Me neither," he whispered as their heads touched. She tried to smile, just for him, but the effort failed. He then took her hands and stood, lifting her to her feet as he did so. She did not hesitate to hug him and kiss and nuzzle his cheek.

Nathan then faced Luke, making sure he kept hold of Chantelle as he did so. "Mister Archer, take us there," he ordered.

"Wh-what?" Luke blubbered.

"Take us, the two of us, there, where it happened. Now." His anger was coming to the fore, growing more intense; Chantelle strengthened her grip on him, giving him even more courage and keeping him calm enough to function. They were operating as one, their lives now so intertwined that Luke felt his daughter slip that little bit further away from him.

"I don't… I d-don't th-think…" Luke stammered. "M-maybe Francis sh-should…"

"No," Nathan interrupted, not even looking at his father for so much as an instant. "Not him. You."

"Dad," Chantelle begged. "Please."

Luke grimaced and nodded slowly. "Yeah, maybe we should…" He tried not to stare at Francis but couldn't help it. The lawyer looked like he had aged a decade or more while telling their children about that terrible September night twenty-one years ago.

"I've got a question, though," Chantelle said suddenly, her grip on Nathan holding fast.

"Yes, sweetheart?" Luke could not keep the tone of hope out of his voice.

"What exactly was the ritual for?" She looked down. "Mister Coulter said it was power and influence, but, really, what was it for?"

"To get that which was our greatest desire," Luke offered lamely.

"Your desire?"

"On successful completion of the ritual, the greatest desire would be achieved." Even as he said it, he knew how ridiculous it all sounded. "Ours was power and influence."

"Mine was that it had never happened," Francis whispered sadly, watching his fingers and nothing else.

Nathan's body stiffened, and Chantelle shifted her arm around his waist, trying to get him to relax, if that was even possible.

"Then the fucking thing worked," he stated coldly. The other three all looked at him with some shock, but he only had eyes for the girl with him, and his tone softened as he went on, "Don't you get it? The greatest desire. It wasn't my dad's, it wasn't your dad's and the rest. It ended up being hers."

"Sorry," Chantelle whispered with a shake of her head.

He placed another soft kiss on her forehead, noting that it was not as warm as it had been. "What do you think she would have wanted at that moment?" he asked her gently. "What would have been her greatest desire?"

She looked at him for a long time, then dropped her eyes and shifted so that she could hold him with both arms, tight and comfortable, protected and protecting. She knew the answer, and she could see in their fathers that they did as well. The greatest desire the ritual had promised had indeed been Chelsea's. Not the want for power and influence to be exercised by a group of confused boys, not Francis's want for the past to have been changed; no, it was all for Chelsea Hartog and her deepest, most desperate and final want:

Revenge.

1991

As usual for a Monday afternoon, the first day of the week, the university cafeteria was crowded. Troy and Francis sat at a table drinking coffee in virtual silence, just watching the people coming and going. September already, and yet the complaints of their first month of tertiary education were still there, topping a list that was being added to every week. They all felt like helpless little fish in a large pond that didn't care if they were eaten or ignored. All their efforts to try to exert any sort of influence like they had at high school had been met by brick walls and withering defeats. They simply did not matter, first-year undergraduate students, several of them still struggling with grades in their chosen courses, despite being deep into the second semester.

They felt their entire lives were at the whims of an overbearing bureaucracy, and, with the possible exception of Francis, they all struggled to cope. High school meant nothing once they were here and studying and attempting to take those first unsteady steps into the real world.

The members of the Round Table missed that control and power they had had, now even more than at the start of the year. The few personal and private things to be discovered about lecturers and tutors were hardly the sorts of things to be used to their advantage. And their increasingly cynical attitude towards everything affected their relationships with their fellow students. This was certainly not how they had imagined university to be.

Francis looked at Troy and scowled a little. The man was in an almost permanent funk nowadays, but there was little he could do to help. And, truth be told, he sometimes felt he could not be bothered. Francis knew he was probably the only one of them coping well, especially with interpersonal relationships. Then again, how much of that was due to his close friendship with Chelsea and how much his own personality even he did not want to actually know.

He shook his head; just being with Troy was bringing him down.

"So, you coming over tonight for a game of *Paranoia*?" Troy asked casually, breaking into his train of thought.

"Don't think so. Sorry," Francis replied.

"And why not this time?" Suspicion clouded Troy's words.

"I promised Chelsea I'd help her read her lines," he responded. "Auditions are on Friday for the undergrad play. I know it's still Monday, but she's panicking a bit."

"Oh, that's right... Chelsea's more important than your friends, isn't she?" Troy sneered.

"Well, she doesn't act like..." He didn't finish.

"Like what?" Troy goaded. "Come on, out with it. Like what?"

"Like a little kid," Francis growled. "Like a spoiled little brat. Your jealousy, mate, is really starting to grate."

Troy stared at him, then said with a malicious grin, "So, can I ask? Is she your girlfriend? Or is she just using you to get good grades?"

"None of your fucking business." Chelsea's voice cut through the air like a knife as she stormed over to the pair of them and, in a big show, draped her arms over Francis's shoulders and planted a long, lingering kiss on his mouth while his hands cupped her buttocks almost automatically.

Troy rolled his eyes and shook his head as they finally disengaged. "Ready?" she asked breathlessly.

"Oh, yeah," he smiled.

"Hmph. Well, enjoy your reading," Troy sneered.

"And the sex afterward," Chelsea added with a deliberately provocative grin. "Oh, we will."

"What?" Troy stared at her while Francis looked away, embarrassed.

"You heard, you little pissant," she returned sharply. "I willingly sleep with Francis. We might not be officially dating, but I like him, and I like his company, and I like him holding me naked when we're finished." She turned to the man in question. "And I really like that you obviously haven't told anyone about us, like you promised, even after all this time. You are so wonderful." Their kiss was passionate, and their eyes met with more than mere friendship.

"You slut." Troy's gaze was hard and direct, his words shattering their mood as effectively as a slap.

"At least Franky here doesn't need to get a girl plastered to sleep with her," Chelsea shot back. Francis faced her, stunned, the question of what she was talking about hanging on his lips.

"How dare you..." Troy got in first. His face turned a bright purple-crimson, and the veins in his neck stood out like tree roots.

"Look, Franky, I don't know about this," Chelsea said suddenly, turning her attention to the man in her arms. "I mean, I like you, I really like you, and everything, but some of your friends are just plain creepy."

Troy started to say something, but Francis's hand silenced him. "Chelsea, I can't choose between you and my friends. We've been mates for years. But you are really special to me. That's unfair..."

"Unfair?" She pondered that for a few moments. "Sure. And I'm sorry, but that's it. Me or them. Think about it. And I guess I'll know your response if I see you at my place some time today or tonight." She kissed him on the mouth, and there was no denying the passion in the action. "Please, really think about it."

Furtive glances from other students watched as one of the most beautiful women on campus walked quickly away from one of the nerds, face low, cheeks tear-streaked. It would later be described to authorities as an apparent lovers' tiff, and it did not seem to make sense to any of them.

"So, what's it going to be?" Troy whispered in Francis's ear.

"I don't know," he whimpered pathetically. "I really

don't know. I've never met anyone like her before, and I don't think I will again. But you guys have been my friends for so long. It's not fair. Why should I have to choose?"

Troy mulled something over in his mind. Then: "We want you with us," he said. "The rest of us, we were going to try another ritual out of that book, a big one, the biggest, a ritual to get our greatest desire, and ours is power. Join us." Troy's smile was sly.

"Why wasn't I told before?"

"Because of her." Troy jerked his thumb in the direction of the retreating girl, barely visible outside through the large glass wall. "You in?"

He shrugged. There was still a way out. He would go to Chelsea's house tonight. Secrets had been kept before; they could be again. He finally nodded.

"Good. We'll do it this weekend, maybe even sooner." He slapped his friend on the shoulder. "It'll be all right." He grabbed his bag and swung it to his shoulder. "Now I've got something to organize before then."

"Yeah, sure." Francis sat back down and watched Troy jog out of the cafeteria. Something was happening that felt very, very wrong, and yet… and yet…

Unfortunately, it also felt so very right.

Chapter Twenty-Two

2012

Francis walked slowly and with some reluctance up the front path of the large suburban house and knocked firmly on the door. It only took a few moments before Julian cautiously pulled it open. When he saw who it was, he swung it wide and ushered Francis inside quickly, looking furtively all about as he did so. Barely had he got inside than Julian shut and locked the door once more.

"Where is everyone?" Francis asked before any greeting could be exchanged.

"Randolph and Sean are with Brandon at the hospital. I've got Allan here with us," he said. "Why? Where's your lad?"

Francis sighed heavily and walked away from his friend down the hallway of the house, soon coming to the dining room. Karyn—her face still bruised, but not as swollen—and her younger brother, Brock, were there, along with Julian's wife, Angela, and young Allan Cornelius, his leg bandaged tight, looking so lost and alone in a strange house with strange people it was almost heart-breaking. In the middle of the table were three take-away pizza boxes, Angela standing over one with a knife to cut some of the slices narrower. She smiled at Francis, but the gesture was hollow and defeated. "Want some?" she asked.

"No thanks," Francis returned before facing Julian. "Can we talk?"

"Sure. Come on." All niceties were dispensed with; this was serious. He led him through the back door to a wide back deck with too much outdoor furniture and a large jacuzzi covered by a piece of blue plastic. Middle-class opulence, it all looked so calm, so normal.

Francis suddenly felt out of place.

He stood at the railing of the deck, looking over a backyard with its cubby house, its play equipment, its bike left outside, its leaves blown across the lawn. Just another suburban home, nothing untoward here; how could this be anything but ordinary? How could every-thing happening actually be happening?

Julian stood beside him. "You look like absolute shit. So, what's going on?" No mincing words, and for that Francis was grateful.

Francis closed his eyes and bowed his head. "Luke's with our kids. They're…they're going for a drive," he muttered evasively.

"Look, Francis, please tell me what's going on. We're all on edge here, and I honestly don't know how much more we can go through before we all just lose it." Julian was begging, near tears. This was wearing on him, but Francis only hoped that he realized he was not alone and that only together could they get through this.

Just like he should have realized things were far from right when Troy had killed himself.

But hindsight made wonderful prophets of them all.

"I told Nathan and Chantelle everything that happened," he whispered, watching but not really seeing a cat skulking across the grass. "Every single thing. Every detail. So, Luke's taking them up there, where it all went down." He grimaced. "It was Nathan's idea."

Julian stared at him with wide, wet eyes. "Buh… but…but why?" He shook his head when Francis started to answer. "No, don't. Don't explain."

Francis turned and looked back at the house. "If we'd told the truth back then…" He swept his arms out. "…none of this, none of our lives, none of our careers, not even our kids… Shit, man, none of this would have happened." He sounded as though their lives for the last two decades were a bad thing.

"We were successful, weren't we?" Julian said wistfully.

"I know," Francis returned quietly. "But at what cost?"

"What?" He shook his head. "It was twenty-one years ago. Twenty-one! And you're only now having qualms? What we did was just a stupid, childish…"

"For fuck's sake, it was not just a stupid, childish prank! How can we reconcile that piece of bullshit with what we actually did? It doesn't make sense!"

Julian turned away from his home. "We can't turn the past back now," he hissed.

"No," Francis agreed. "Our kids certainly wouldn't want that, would they?"

Julian gritted his teeth as he tried desperately to keep his emotions under control. "That's not fair," he growled. "Besides, what's happening to our kids…"

"…has nothing to do with Chelsea Hartog?" Francis finished cruelly. "You know better than that. You've already admitted it. Don't go back on me now." They stared at one another, neither able to say a thing. Julian blinked first and turned his head. Francis took no pleasure in it.

"What can we do then?" Julian asked hoarsely, looking through the back door at the family around the table, eating their pizza as though it was the most onerous chore on Earth.

"Be honest." Francis groaned loudly at his own suggestion and thumped the railing hard enough to reverberate through the decking. "If only we'd been honest back then, then…"

"As you said, though, none of this would have happened," Julian countered, trying to turn around the point Francis had already made. "We'd have been in prison, we'd never have met our wives. And we would never have had our children." His voice dropped. "This world, our world, would be so incredibly different."

"So, you're saying what we did was worth it in the end?" There was no emotion in the voice, just a simple, loaded question.

"No, no, never," Julian responded nervously. "What we did afterward, though… That…"

"Dad!" There was such incredible terror in that one screamed word.

His eyes widened. "Karyn!"

Without even thinking, the two men raced to the back door and shoved it open, then bolted inside. Julian grabbed Allan and swung the horrified child up into his uninjured arm and away from the table while Francis tackled Angela to the ground, the knife in her hands clattering to the floor, and all the while Karyn and Brock screamed wildly.

Angela turned her head, and Francis gasped.

Those eyes, that mouth, that golden aura of hair.

"Why, Franky, why?" the face of Chelsea whispered huskily.

And then it was Angela once more, her lower lip trembling, her eyes tearing, her whole body shaking. "What… What…?" she tried, but her gaze fell on the knife, and she burst into heaving sobs.

"Daddy, why did mummy try to…?" Brock started to ask, but he didn't have the words to succinctly express what he'd seen: his mother leaning across the table, her chest crushing one of the pizzas, the knife held in her hand like a poor man's version of *Psycho*, aiming for the young boy now held by her husband.

Angela pushed Francis roughly off and sprinted to the other end of the house. A door banged open, and the sound of her violently throwing up reached them.

Francis looked helplessly at Julian. He was just staring back, ignoring the child in his arms, who squirming frantically to get away from these people he didn't know, the pain from his damaged hip clearly running through him like an electrical storm.

"What was… Why did… Holy fuck, what just happened?" Julian finally whispered in panic.

"You saw it. You must have seen it," Francis uttered softly.

"Wha…what do we do?" Julian whined. "She was here! She was… She was…was *in* Angela!"

"Lemme go! Lemme go! Lemme go!" the boy in Julian's arms suddenly squealed.

"Shit," Julian groaned, setting the child down on his back on the floor, where he rolled over and crawled away, dragging his injured limb behind him as though it weighed more than the rest of his body together. The professor watched him go, then looked up as he heard his wife throw up once more, followed by loud, gut-wrenching sobs that echoed throughout the rest of the house. His own children were also crying and staring at him, the man they knew and loved a stranger to their eyes, their mother just as bad.

In less than five minutes, his entire family had been damaged, maybe beyond repair.

Just like that.

"Worth it," he mumbled pathetically, rubbing his still-bandaged shoulder. "So worth it." Karyn slid out of her seat, away from him, and took her brother by the hand, the lad never once taking his eyes from his father. They crouched down near Allan, and he went directly to the teenager and curled up in her lap, weeping softly, while Brock hid behind her.

Francis finally stood. "Call the others. We're going to go up with Luke and the kids." He looked at the three on the floor. They shrank back. "And for their safety, we should bring Karyn and Allan as well."

"What? We can't... and Brock... I should stay... Angela..."

Francis ran his hand over his face; Julian was losing his grip on reality right before his very eyes. He strode across to the man who was a doctor of physics and grabbed his wounded shoulder.

"Fuck!" he screamed. "What was that for?" The children winced again.

"You back with me now?" Francis growled.

Julian stared at him, rubbing the wound carefully, then dropped his head. "Sorry," he sighed. "What do we have to do?"

"Call the others. Get them to meet us up there." He looked at the youngsters on the floor. "I'll get Brock to stay here and get the other two in the car."

"No..." Karyn whispered.

Francis squatted but didn't move closer to them. "Why not?"

"What mum did was..." she started, then paused. "What happened?" she asked. Brock hid his face behind her, but Allan watched Francis curiously.

"You do know that wasn't your mother that did... that just did that, don't you?" he asked carefully, deliberately using a leading question.

"But I saw..." she tried to explain, then stopped. Francis was looking at her quizzically, like her math teacher when she knew Karyn had the answer. The degree of familiarity, however small, made the connection that important a bit easier. "That wasn't mum's face," she finally said. She cocked her head to one side. "She was beautiful. Who was she?"

"She's..." He sighed again and shook his head. "She's someone we knew a long time ago." He risked inching forward. "Now, you need to... We are asking you to help us, please, so she won't do anything to anyone again."

"But how could she be on mum's face? That's like, not real." The language was youthful, the sentiment, adult. Francis was relieved.

"I know," he sighed. "Lots of things that are happening can't be real, yet, unfortunately, they are. But I need your help now to stop it. Please, Karyn." He smiled. "Oh, and I think it's time you met my son. He's Captain of your school, and right now he's trying to stop this. What do you say?"

"How can I help?"

"If we've got all of you together, we know exactly where she's going to be, so we can...well, we can face her." He was thinking on his feet, but it made sense. Wasn't that their original reasoning in gathering the kids all in one place? It had been to keep their children easier to watch, but was there also the concept to attract trouble... Was this really the right thing to do?

"I don't understand," she murmured.

"I know. And I know you don't know me, and what I'm asking is pretty big, and that is that you trust me. Please."

She stared at him for what felt like a long time. The child-like panic was replaced by the surprisingly profound wisdom of the fifteen-year-old she was. Then: "Dad said that at school you were the one friend everyone knew they could trust. My dad was the one who could organize, Allan's dad could write anything, all the rest. But you... So, yes... I'll trust you because dad trusts you."

Francis managed a smile, casting a quick glance at Julian, questioning his description of his abilities as a youth. He turned back to Karyn. "Good," he said. "But I need to be honest here. This is going to be... Well, it's going to be scary."

"Is it going to help dad as well?"

Francis shrugged sadly. "I don't know," he finally whispered.

She nodded. "Good answer," she replied. "I think I can trust you as well." She paused, collecting her thoughts. "So, what do you want me to do?" Fifteen going on twenty-one was how Julian had described her to him, and Francis thanked the powers that be that that was the case.

1991

Francis felt a hand yank him back even as Troy let himself fall forward.

The sound was surprisingly soft.

Chelsea's head was thrown backward.

"No…" Francis whimpered. "No…"

Her eyes searched him out, wide and pleading. She reached a trembling hand across to him as the first bubble of blood burst at the corner of her mouth and ran down the side of her chin, scarlet drops striking her torso like red tears. The point of the knife was visible near the center of her chest, between her breasts, the crimson stain on her white clothing growing larger and larger with each and every slowing heartbeat.

"F-F-F…," she tried to say. His hand stretched forward. Their fingers touched.

Luke and Brandon struck as one. The first blade slid into her midsection, the next into her hip. Blood erupted, living lava gushing forth. Luke looked down at what he had done, at the handle of the weapon quaking in her stomach with each forced breath, and turned and dry-retched loudly.

The hand let go of Francis, and Julian moved across. He just jabbed forward, almost blindly. His knife penetrated her lower neck and shoulder with an explosive fountain of red that struck Troy in the face, making his grin widen maniacally.

Chelsea's eyes fluttered and closed for the final time.

Her fingers fell away from Francis.

"No…" Francis repeated.

Randolph looked at the others, gritted his teeth, and just drove the knife in his hands forward. It struck her wrist, but the blood that flowed out had less pressure than they would have expected, coming out in pathetic pulses of thickening fluid.

Chelsea's mouth fell open. Francis was sure he heard a word come from her lips like the wind across a field of dead grass. He only wished he had heard her final utterance, to know the last thing on her mind… if only…

Suddenly, in a brief frenzy, Sean slashed sideways, ripping open her throat. He then rammed the weapon into the gaping wound, coloring the entire upper half of the white clothing a deep, almost purple crimson.

"Now! Before she's dead!" Troy yelled furiously.

"What?" Francis was in shock.

"Shit!" Troy growled and leaped at him, landing on him like a wounded animal. He grabbed the knife from Francis's belt and shoved it into his hand. Francis's fingers grasped it on instinct. "Now, you bastard!" Troy demanded

Francis shook his head meekly.

Troy grabbed his arm and lifted it.

Francis found the mental strength to fight against it.

Sean then leaned on him as well.

He was moving, despite his best efforts. He twisted his body as he fell.

The knife entered her smooth, milky flesh, severing the femoral artery in her upper leg as messily as any other wound on her battered body. Her blood burst forth and struck him in the face, a sticky mess that assailed his nostrils and matted his hair and was her.

It was Chelsea.

He jerked his head around quickly.

In front of his eyes, her own bloodied face filled his vision; it was all he could see.

Chelsea gasped once. One last time.
Then everything was still.
And red.
And changed.
Forever.

Chapter Twenty-Three

2012

Nathan's and Chantelle's hands remained tightly entwined as they slowly followed Luke through the trees, guided only by the single beam of his old flashlight.

"This hasn't stayed the same," Luke muttered absently. "I thought it might."

"Twenty-one years, dad," Chantelle stated, squeezing Nathan's hand as she spoke. "Of course, it's changed."

Chantelle's finger-grip remained strong. Nathan saw more than a hint of worry cross her face. The man with them was not the confident teacher who had brought her up in a loving and caring home. This was a nervous wreck whose eyes darted about like a frightened rabbit, a man who had done simply what he had been told and so had come out here with barely an argument to face his own fears and past without question.

"Ahh, here's something." Luke's voice had gained a note of confidence.

Nathan and Chantelle felt their throats constrict and moved in closer together. "Here's what?" Nathan asked, trying to keep himself in control.

"The track. Look." He shone the torch down to illuminate a river-smoothed stone about the size of four fists, then to their left another about five paces away. "Your father did that. I never really understood why this was the path he made, but I think it was the way he found his way to come back here so no-one else could." He paused and finally looked at the teenagers. "Well, at least once a year, anyway, I reckon," he added as an afterthought, as though it meant nothing.

Without further word, they followed the path of rocks. Some had been moved over the years, and some had been overgrown by the grass or covered by the forest detritus, but soon enough they found themselves at the edge of a small copse.

"Holy shit," Luke mumbled.

Nathan and Chantelle rushed to his side. The grass of the clearing looked like it had actually been cut, and relatively recently, too. Years of fallen branches were piled up on the sides, along with leaves and small saplings, creating a natural wall, sort of like a beaver's dam. And standing proudly in the middle was a cairn of small stones about a meter high.

"What's all this?" Nathan asked quietly.

"I don't know. It wasn't like this the last time I was here," Luke responded, his voice distant, shocked.

"When was that, dad?"

Luke did not answer for a long time, and when he

spoke, it was as though he were in a dream. "It was nineteen years ago. You were still a baby. I came here on September nineteenth, the anniversary. The second anniversary. I was here the year before as well, but that second time… Yeah. Francis was here. Brandon, too. I think Julian might have turned up as well. We didn't say anything. It felt too wrong. I knew I wasn't coming back. I had you, I had a real family. Julian must've left first. Brandon and I went together. We left Francis here. I'll bet he comes here every year, though. I mean, look at this place."

"He really, truly loved her, didn't he?" Nathan whispered, his voice hoarse, cracking with emotion.

"Yeah, he really did," Luke said. "If Troy hadn't jumped him, he never would have… Shit, he was forced into this. And I reckon he really has lived this every day of his life."

"Mum said when they divorced she thought he was involved with another woman," Nathan said. "I never believed her, but then I never would have guessed it was a dead girl."

Those final, blunt words made Luke jump a little, his body becoming tense. "Well, let's go," he murmured, speaking quickly, obviously eager to leave the place.

"Where?' Chantelle asked.

"Well, this is where we… where… where… you know." Luke was barely holding it together.

"Where she actually died?" Nathan tried.

He nodded slowly. Chantelle was sure she could see a tear on his cheek. "But I think Francis wants us to find her. The real her."

The two youngsters looked at one another. "She's not here?" Chantelle whispered.

Luke shook his head. "We took her," he whispered. "She was still in the bag. We zipped it up again and carried her off." He touched Nathan's arm. "Francis didn't come. He stayed right here, in the darkness. He wouldn't even clean her blood off his face.

"Hell, that poor girl spent three days in a bag at Troy's place—he had a room out the back and his parents simply never went out there—and he said he let her go to the toilet and fed her, but I don't think he did. She said he didn't, anyway. He made her change into that white nightdress, and I think he might've taken advantage of her as well. Don't know for sure, but… Well, yeah, then we brought her out here and… well, you know what we did. And then we dumped her like yesterday's garbage, in a garbage bag."

He turned then and strode away, the flashlight finding each rock as though guided there.

Chantelle and Nathan stayed where they were.

There was something about this place, especially as it gained the blue glow of night when Luke disappeared down the rocky trail. It was strangely calm, a well of quiet in a world that no longer made sense.

Nathan's and Chantelle's hands moved so that they allowed their arms to slide around one another's waists.

Under different circumstances, the place could even have been said to possess an allure, a sense of calm. They squeezed one another briefly, then Chantelle placed a soft kiss on his cheek. He even managed a smile.

Neither of them considered where they were; the atmosphere was no longer that of a graveyard, a memorial to death. It was their place now; nothing else mattered, just this tiny pocket and one another.

A white mist started to form, spreading across the ground, a low-lying cloud, soft, like the last remnants of the smoke of the campfire, the down from the wings of an angel. It added to the atmosphere, giving it an other-worldly texture, like a dream made solid.

It swirled around a little in a breeze neither could feel, circling about the cairn, becoming thicker, covering the stones, looking like a statue made of the very air itself.

"It's beautiful," Chantelle whispered. Nathan smiled and kissed her forehead in agreement. Their embrace was organic, their kiss was lingering.

The aura they could detect was filled with love, not with the death and horror and loss that this place, hidden away for over two decades, represented to their fathers.

They parted, their eyes remaining fixed on one another, their smiles slight but sincere.

A movement on the very edge of their vision caught their attention. They turned quickly, the mood evaporating, though not completely. Chantelle giggled in embarrassment and was about to suggest maybe it was an owl or something when there was another darting motion, this one more definite.

And definitely made by something larger than an owl.

"Where's Dad?" Chantelle suddenly whispered.

Nathan didn't get a chance to reply.

She stepped out from behind the cairn, rising to her full height like a flower opening itself to the morning sun. If anything, the photographs in the old yearbooks and on the Internet and the brief glimpses already afforded them had understated her beauty, the lustrous golden hair that was draped over her shoulders and covered her chest appearing like a halo of heavenly light, the perfect and unblemished skin seemingly made out of the purest marble.

And her smile… It was sweet and innocent, the smile of a goddess.

She opened her arms wide, and everything about her was so welcoming. Chantelle's hand dropped and took Nathan's; he responded by pulling her in right beside him. Neither could take their eyes from the personification of beauty in front of them.

Her mouth opened and the word, "Come," floated to them on a wind that didn't exist.

Chantelle began to step forward first.

Nathan hesitated, then took one slow step toward her.

Another movement distracted his attention.

His father was standing there. His eyes were wide with fear, and he was shaking his head violently from side to side.

Coldness wafted over Nathan, and he spun to gaze at Chantelle. Now drifting lightly across the grass toward the woman and her wide, outstretched arms.

"No," he whispered.

He took two steps and jumped as the white, glowing arms closed up. He tackled Chantelle about the waist and pulled her to the ground, both crying out as they landed. Nathan could feel the wetness from Chantelle's stomach leak alarmingly over his arm; his own leg was a mass of pure agony, and he could not bear to look at it to see what extra damage he had caused.

"What the hell was…" Chantelle began, rounding on him as well as she could, but the words became stuck in her throat. Her eyes grew larger, her jaw fell open, her lips quivered.

Nathan spun around and fell to his back, resisting the temptation to push himself away on his throbbing, pained leg. Instead, he groped for and found Chantelle's hand yet again and held on tight. He was not abandoning her now.

The woman was now standing with her hands folded across her stomach, her eyes squeezed shut, her mouth set into a grim line. And there was blood. Blood flowed from her shoulder, neck, chest, wrist, stomach, hip, and leg. It covered almost all of her white clothing in a glowing scarlet that moved and rippled over her perfect form, a separate entity living all over her.

The eyes and mouth shot open.

Blood, So much blood. Too much blood.

The blood poured from them in a neverending waterfall, pooling on the ground at her feet in an ocean of putrefying body liquids.

Chantelle screamed.

The mouth twisted into a malicious grin as the blood-filled eyes narrowed and the arms were thrown wide once again in a welcoming, warming, wanting embrace.

***

"Here," Luke mumbled.

"Here," Julian agreed.

The other three just looked down at the creek bed, a channel that clearly had not held water in many years.

"Here? Exactly here?" Sean whispered tentatively.

"I don't really remember now," Luke said, his voice still vague, his eyes distant.

It was Brandon who knelt down and started to claw at the soft earth with his bare hands.

The others soon joined him, even Julian with only one usable arm.

Just over twenty-one years earlier they had done this already; then it had been digging into the bottom of a flowing creek, going down until they had struck too much rocky material.

That was to conceal.

Now it was time to reveal.

***

"Stop! Please, please stop!"

Francis ran across the small field and stood between the strange, horrific apparition and the teenagers. Chantelle threw herself at Nathan and cowered against him, hiccupping in terror and pain.

The blood-drenched woman stared at him, the grin curling into a scowl. The eyes stopped crying their crimson tears; the blood slowed as it dribbled over her bright lips.

"Chelsea, please," Francis begged. He showed her his hands, submissively, openly, honestly. "Please, Chelsea. Please."

Her gaze narrowed even further. Her arms were slowly lowered until they were by her sides, palms facing forwards. The flow of blood from the seven wounds slowed to a congealing trickle.

"It was never meant to be like this," Francis whispered. "I always loved you." He shifted sideways far enough to touch the top of the cairn. "I never ever forgot you."

Nathan recognized the opportunity his father was giving him. He forced himself to his feet, the blood gushing out of his wound as soon as he put his weight on the leg. He reached down to Chantelle; she didn't need to be asked twice as she grabbed his wrist and struggled to stand beside him, clutching her abdomen tenderly. "Come on," he whispered and virtually dragged her away.

They stopped short. Karyn held Allan in her arms, the young boy sobbing against her neck, and stared at them, scared beyond words, but unwilling to move.

"Who's..." Chantelle started, but Nathan touched her shoulder.

"What are you doing here, Karyn?" he asked quietly, gently, kindly.

"How do you know…?" she began to ask, fear touching her words, but then she shook her head. It wasn't important. What was important was that this was happening and it could not be real. Red women, (*bleeding?*), strange clearings in forests, her mum possessed. Not real. But this guy was, and he was here, and she was sure she had seen him at school; there was only one person this could be. "Your dad brought us." She could not help but look past Nathan at the glowing red, white, and gold woman. "He said he needed all of us here to stop this. What's going on?"

Nathan carefully touched her bruised face and turned her attention back to him and Chantelle. "I don't know," he said, "but if my dad wants us here, then I'll stay."

She swallowed hard and held tightly onto Allan. "Are we going to be okay?" she asked.

Nathan sighed and set himself. "Yes," he stated simply. He then slowly turned around to look at the center of the copse and its two occupants, carefully moving Chantelle behind him as he did so. "Yes," he repeated, "you will all be okay." His choice of words did not go unnoticed, and Chantelle wrapped her arms about him from behind, glad he could not see her crying this time.

Francis, though, did not notice anything. He only had eyes for the woman in white. The flight of the teenagers, the gathering of the children, none of it seemed to matter. Just the woman. He lifted his hand from the cairn and reached reached out to her. His fingers touched the blood-soaked cheek. It was cold and smooth, like stone.

Then her eyes suddenly shifted, gazing upwards.

***

"Holy fuck, she's still here!"

Brandon scuttled backward, unable to draw his eyes from the smallish hole they had created.

And from the thick, black plastic bag at the bottom of it.

The others just gaped at it, unable to say anything.

It was Julian who resumed digging, his one useful arm churning like a machine.

Before long, all five were once more going at it, uncovering more and more plastic, trying hard not to think about what it contained.

Who it contained.

***

The blood stopped flowing from all wounds, but Francis noticed with unease that the holes in her body remained open and gaping.

His hand moved slightly so that the palm cupped her cheek as though the blood was not even there. He allowed himself the hint of a smile. The stone of her flesh was no longer marble, no longer ice.

She opened her eyes properly, but her mouth remained downturned.

Her body shook a little, a brief tremor that ran

through her whole being, and she blinked twice.

***

The outline of the bag sat there in the soft soil.

"Well?" Brandon asked.

"Yeah, well," Sean muttered in return.

Luke dug out the edge a little more. Then a little more. Small handfuls until his hand wedged between the ground and the soft, pliable side.

The whole thing moved.

"Oh, good God," he squeaked like a child. It still had solidity inside. He peered nervously at the others but stayed where he was.

"Fuck," Julian groaned and did likewise on the other side. The other three did not hesitate before joining them, knowing this had to be done. Too much depended on it.

***

Her mouth moved at the corners.

The coagulating blood trickled slowly and thickly down her body, a thousand crimson caterpillars making their way towards the ground, leaving the skin clean, the garments unstained.

Francis managed a proper smile, one that might even have been genuine.

This was Chelsea. *His* Chelsea.

She leaned her head into his hand and closed her eyes. The warmth of her flesh was increasing. He touched her chin with his other hand. "Please, Chelsea," he whispered.

The eyelids fluttered. The eyes themselves were slightly cloudy, but there was complete recognition.

"Franky."

The voice was hoarse, croaking, spoken as if the words had been forced out through disused and damaged muscles.

"Why?" Francis whispered.

She shook her head. Her gaze shifted over his shoulder.

He slowly turned his head, then could not help but gasp.

She was staring directly at his son, standing uneasily on one leg in front of the rest of the children, defiantly, firmly, bravely…exactly the way he hadn't stood up to his own friends twenty-one years earlier.

"Why not?" The words were formed as the wafting of the wind through the branches of the trees. But that was enough to send a chill up Francis's spine and into the back of his skull.

***

"One, two, three," Brandon counted, and all of them lifted on cue.

The mud beneath the plastic bag tried to hold onto its prize, keeping a firm grip that only the combined strength of the five men could overcome.

The sound as the ground finally let go was that of

tearing, ripping flesh.

Slowly they raised what they had come here for onto the edge of the dead waterway. They all caught their breath, and it was Randolph who said what they were all thinking. "Holy fuck. We've done it."

***

Chelsea lifted her arms. All the scars had closed over, healing so completely that not so much as a line marked that perfect skin. Her eyes stared directly at him, now as clear and bright as the first time he had sat down with her over a high school history book all those years ago. This was the Chelsea he remembered.

The Chelsea he loved.

With a speed that stunned him, she hurled him sideways. He slammed into the pile of stones he had constructed and then cared for for so many years. The landing was painful, and he fell so that too many of the rocks crashed down onto him.

She barely cast him a glance as she strode purposefully forward.

She had but one target...

Nathan stayed his ground, no idea of what he was actually going to do.

She slowed as she neared them. Her smile softened, her body language open and welcome. This was the university student, the popular girl at high school, the tennis champion, the English Literature student, the girl too many men fell in love with at first sight.

"Come, children," she whispered. She held her hands out. "Come with me."

Allan cried louder and pushed his head against Karyn, who hid behind Nathan, while Chantelle moved enough so she could grip his arm tight.

"No," Nathan said firmly.

"I shall get what I most desire," she stated quietly and confidently.

"Revenge?" Nathan asked boldly. Her smile was answer enough. "Or is it what you lost?" he added suddenly.

She stopped, her grin faltering.

Nathan held that cold gaze, eyes that stared through him, into him, beyond him. He forced himself to stand taller and prouder, and he wrapped his arm around Chelsea's shoulders, then kissed her softly on the mouth. She grasped his cheeks and returned it with fervor, hot tears coursing down her face. They separated shortly, yet reluctantly. Nathan removed her hands from his face. "Take these two and go," he told her, finishing with a final kiss to her forehead.

"No," Chantelle sobbed. "Don't..."

That was the response he had expected; no, hoped for. Still, he was already tentatively stepping forward. "Go on," he said, pushing it as far as he thought he could.

"Nathan, please," Chantelle begged.

Chelsea watched the scene, jealousy filling those beautiful features. Her eyes moved past the approaching boy to the weeping girl and back again. Her mouth twitched.

Nathan could feel that she was unsure now. He edged nearer. A subtle movement, cautious and slow, came from behind her. She was distracted by him; this was good.

Nathan stopped and stared into that gorgeous face.

A hand grasped Chelsea's shoulder and forced her to turn around. She did so, but reluctantly, anger now dominating all about her.

Francis brought his face in close to hers.

She stared back.

A moment's hesitation. A moment's anticipation.

Mouths parted. Eyes closed. Bodies relaxed. Lips met.

Francis's hands moved and wrapped themselves in the golden halo of her long, silky hair.

Chelsea's arms tentatively snaked around his waist.

The years fell away. It was the middle of 1991 once more; 2012 was still a future that was not even worth considering. Nathan was sure that the gray streaks in his father's hair faded, that his body became fitter, that his skin smoothed itself.

The kiss became briefly more intense, and then they parted, foreheads resting on one another, the smiles they shared meant for themselves and themselves alone.

The approach of five men bearing a heavy burden went unnoticed by the duo.

"Holy shit," Randolph muttered. "Is that…?"

"Doesn't matter," Julian hissed. "Keep on going. We have to do this."

"But…" Randolph tried. The words did not come.

Brandon slapped his shoulder. He shook his head clear. They finally set the plastic bag down carefully. Julian pulled open a pocket knife and pierced the top of the bag beside the rusted zipper.

Chelsea swung her head to stare at him, her lower lip trembling. She began to shake her head, but Francis turned her face back to him with two fingers and grabbed her with both arms and just held onto her tight. This was the Francis Coulter of 1991; Nathan did not think he could remember seeing his dad look so content before.

Their next kiss was that of teenaged lovers in the process of discovering themselves.

Julian's knife sliced down in one fell motion. He waited a heartbeat and then pulled the sides apart, letting out an invisible cloud of putrid air that made all five men move away hastily.

Chelsea tried to fight against Francis, but he maintained his grip.

"Dad, no… Please, Dad, no…" Nathan gasped. The others merely looked at him, wondering what he was seeing that they weren't.

Francis suddenly grabbed Chelsea even tighter as her legs seemed to give way, stopping her from collapsing. Their lips remained locked together, and they sank to their knees.

A white mist formed around them, obscuring Chelsea's lower limbs, merging with the clothing she wore. The cloud flowed down the sleeves, enveloping her hands and, with them, Francis's body. It grew over him like a spider's web until their faces were the only parts that could be seen clearly in the fog.

"Dad…" Nathan sobbed, so quietly that only Chantelle could hear him. She was at his side straight away and grasped him about the waist, hugging him with as much strength as she could, pressing her head against him, holding him back. "Dad…" he repeated, even softer. All his resistance stopped; he just let Chantelle hold him.

The cloud finally encased them both.

And then it was gone.

Francis was on his side, alone, on the cold, damp grass, completely still.

Nathan was at his side as fast as his bleeding leg could carry him. He lifted his father's head and placed two fingers on the side of his neck. Chantelle's hands came to rest on his shoulders as the crying started in earnest.

Five men looked inside the bag.

The body was no more than a skin-covered skeleton, dressed in rust-stained, torn, white clothing, locks of long golden hair resting beneath the skull.

"Isn't that impossible?" Julian murmured.

"After all this, you're talking impossible?" Brandon whispered before turning his back on the remains. Death was not important; life was all that mattered. He started towards the children. Allan reached for him. He broke into a jog and took the boy from Karyn's arms, and they gripped each other so tightly about the neck they both struggled to get in a decent breath. But that was okay.

Julian took his cue and smiled hopefully at Karyn. Her expression was one of fear, made all the worse by the bruising that discolored her face, but he had moved only a few paces before she had him about the chest, something he was sure she had not done in so many years. His shoulder felt like fire, but his daughter's embrace felt like perfection.

Luke stood. He tried to feel the same happiness as the other two, but it didn't come. It seemed to him, looking at his daughter and her sharing of the grief of a boy they hardly knew, that Chantelle was drifting and… She lifted her head to look at him and gave him a smile that melted his heart as much as it had when she was only fifteen minutes old. Joy…and such sadness. Chantelle's attention returned to Nathan, Luke's to the man before the two of them. No matter what else, today, a good man, a trusted man, a friend had died.

Nothing would ever change that.

A noise behind them made Luke, Brandon, and Julian turn.

Randolph and Sean had gathered six knives, somehow amid their own grief when faced with all the reunions about them they had continued to do what they felt they must. They stared down at the bag and the single knife that remained—the one that rested in the middle of the skeleton's chest.

Brandon rocked Allan back and forth. He looked at his son's still-distraught face, then back at his oldest friends. "I think," he said slowly and carefully, "that Troy admitted to his lawyer that he did something terrible twenty-one years ago. Something to his lawyer's girlfriend." Everyone looked at him, including Nathan.

Chantelle fell against the teenaged boy, her bleeding stomach burning like a fever, but she paid it no heed. Not now. Karyn twisted around to look as well, as much an adult as any of them, the games and pettiness of high school sitting so uneasily in her head at that moment. Brandon pondered his next comments and chose his words carefully. "Francis was distraught. He loved Chelsea. He worked out where Troy had done the deed and came here after Troy's suicide and after all the coincidental accidents," he went on, "and he found the truth. He uncovered… Maybe it was the exertion of what he had done, maybe it was his grief…" He stopped there.

No-one argued.

"Revenge…" the wind whispered.

Nathan placed his father's head gently on the ground and let Chantelle wrap herself around him, both oblivious to their pain.

"Love..." the wind whispered in the same voice. "Love…"

It had come to pass, after all that time.

The greatest desire had been achieved.

ABOUT THE AUTHOR

S. Gepp is an Australian, with two children, a number of university degrees and diplomas, and a resumé that looks like a list of every job you could ever have without really trying, including stints as a school teacher, scientist, editor and journalist. He has also been a performance acrobat, a professional wrestler, a stand-up comedian and an actor. He has been writing for 30 years and hopes to be a real writer if he grows up. A dull life.

And be sure to check out
these other novellas from
Grinning Skull Press

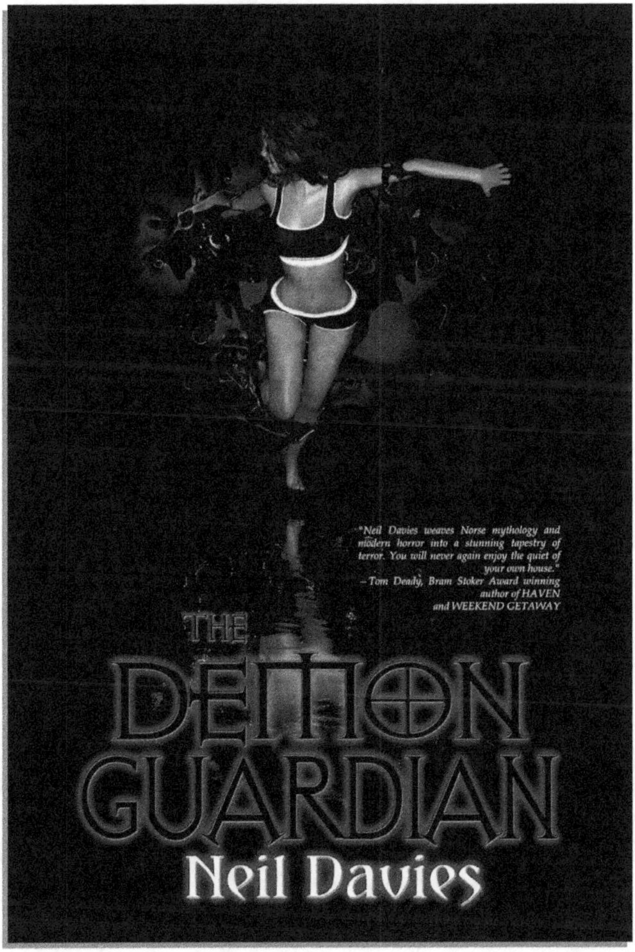

CHAPTER ONE

It was one of those rare mornings when Dennis Parkes woke at peace. Cautiously, he lifted his head, waiting for the quick, shadowy movements seen from the corner of his eye, the sibilant whispering filling the stale air of the small bedroom. There was nothing. Just still, silent darkness.

He thought of waking his wife, Swan, to share his sense of relief and happiness, but she had never heard the voices or seen the shadows move. If he woke her, she would be angry at being disturbed more than an hour before the alarm was due. It would ruin his mood. It would ruin the stillness. He eased his head back onto the pillow and lay awake, enjoying the silence, the peace.

Slowly, dawn lit up the window through the thin curtains, and birdsong twittered and whistled through the trees of nearby Ottmor Wood. If only all mornings could be like this, he would not need the medication, the therapy. It might even make his life with Swan less combative.

If only.

Wyatt Road lay quiet and sleepy on the outskirts of Anbal, a small village on the Wirral Peninsula. The commuter traffic, from Liverpool to the north and Chester to the south, bypassed Anbal on the M53 motorway. What little diverted through the narrow main street of the village itself passed the end of Wyatt Road without any thought of turning in. Wyatt Road was a dead-end. If you didn't live there and were not visiting, your only destination would be the turning circle just before the wooden stile leading to Ottmor Wood.

It was the quiet, more than anything, that had drawn Swanhild Parkes to number 20 when it came up for sale. A narrow mid-terraced house, it stood more or less equidistant between the end of the road and the wood. Built in the early 1930s, it had more-recent additions of a concrete driveway at the front, newly installed plumbing and electrics, and a narrow, but long, well-groomed garden at the back. That was eleven years ago, when she had persuaded Dennis that this should be their first family home. Now, standing at the kitchen sink, staring at the overgrown lawn, the legs of upturned plastic chairs like skeletal limbs reaching up from the long grass, she felt nothing but despair.

"It's not my fault I got made redundant," shouted

Dennis from somewhere behind her. She had almost forgotten they were mid-argument. The same argument they had had almost weekly for the last three years.

"No," she said, agreeing. "But it is your fault that the grass hasn't been cut for weeks."

"You know it hurts my back."

"We can't afford to get someone in anymore," she said, striving to be both truthful and understanding. "Since you can't do it, *I'll* have to do it at the weekend."

"I'll worry if you do that. I don't want you to do that."

His voice almost whined. She hated it when he whined.

"Yes, well, there's not much choice, is there?" She turned from the sink to face her husband. "Now, I have to get to work."

"I'll move the car," said Dennis. "May as well go to the shop while I'm out."

He turned and began burrowing through the accumulated clutter under the stairs for his shoes.

Swan wanted to be even more truthful. She wanted to tell her husband that he was a morbidly obese, out-of-work man in his early forties, and that it was no wonder his back and joints hurt, given the weight they were carrying. But she knew the redundancy had hurt him badly, destroyed his confidence, shoved him into depression, and that the weight gain was almost completely due to emotional eating since then. He was not currently fit for work, mentally or physically. She wanted to tell him these things, but she knew it would just deepen his depression and worsen an already terrible self-image. He needed to know she supported him, still loved him, despite all that had happened.

Dennis had found his shoes and, with some difficulty, put them on. Breathing heavily, he led the way out of the front door. Swan shrugged on her one and only coat and followed.

Dennis reversed his old Peugeot 405 out of the narrow driveway and waited, the engine idling. He felt comfortable in the car, able to relax, away from whispered voices, away from Swan. Alone. It had been bought for the long drive to his last place of work, and he held on to it stubbornly after the redundancy. Big and impractical it might be, given how little driving he now did, but it was *his*. And it was the only thing that connected him to his old life. His purposeful, *employed* life. When he hadn't felt quite so worthless. When he didn't spend days in introspection and deepening depresssion. When he felt confident his wife loved him.

Swan's Vauxhall Corsa reversed out, and the bright pink of the bodywork pulled a slight smile out of his frown. Even she agreed she bought it more for the colour than the car itself.

They waved to each other as she drove off, and Dennis waited until he saw her safely negotiate the junction at the end of the road before he put the Peugeot into gear and headed for the shops.

Just get the essentials and back home.

But did he really want to be home? There was nothing there but an empty house, another long day of watching the clock ticking slowly by, the flash of movement from the corner of his eye—and the voices.

He wanted to tell Swan, he really did. But how do you tell your wife that you hear voices in the home you share? She already thought him fat and useless, blamed him for his depression and for failing to get another job. To admit to hearing voices and seeing things would finally convince her he was completely insane. She would probably leave. He couldn't risk that.

Only two other people knew about the voices and the shadows: his local general practitioner, Dr. Banks, and his one and only friend, Travis Newman. The only two people he had told differed in their reactions.

"It's not that unusual," Dr. Banks had said. "Particularly in someone suffering from clinical depression, like yourself."

"But what do the voices mean?" said Dennis. "Why are they mostly unintelligible? Shouldn't they be sending me messages from God or something?"

Dr. Banks smiled. "The mind is a complex thing," he said. "It can push bad and unpleasant thoughts aside if it doesn't want to deal with them. It separates them, and they become a different part of you."

"You mean like another person in my head?"

"Not quite, but another aspect of you, certainly." Dr. Banks removed his narrow-framed glasses and held them in his right hand, twisting them back and forth as he spoke. "These are things you don't want to have to cope with just now, so they're pushed into the background. And mostly, that's where they stay. But every now and then they push back, and that's where the voices are coming from."

"So it's all in my mind," said Dennis. "Does this mean I'm psychotic or something?"

Dr. Banks shook his head. "No. It's not any kind of psychosis. It's *dissociation*. Like I said, it's quite common among those suffering from depression."

Travis, on the other hand, saw things slightly differently.

"So, you hear voices. Are they always in your head, or sometimes from outside?"

They had been sitting in their local Sainsburys cafe, meeting up during Travis's lunch break from his nearby office job, and before Dennis went shopping. Talking with Travis boosted Dennis's self-confidence enough to make it round the aisles without panicking.

"Sometimes in my head, sometimes not," said Dennis, keeping his voice low. He was sure some of the old people at neighbouring tables were listening.

"I don't reckon it's anything to do with depression," said Travis, casually dismissing what Dennis had told him about the doctor's opinion. "I think it's a lot simpler than all that stuff."

"Oh yes?" said Dennis, doubtfully. As a general rule, he sided with doctors over laymen, but he always had time for Travis's thoughts on matters, however outrageous they might turn out to be. "And so what do you think it is?"

"Simple." Travis leaned closer, lowering his voice to a whisper. "Your house is *haunted*."

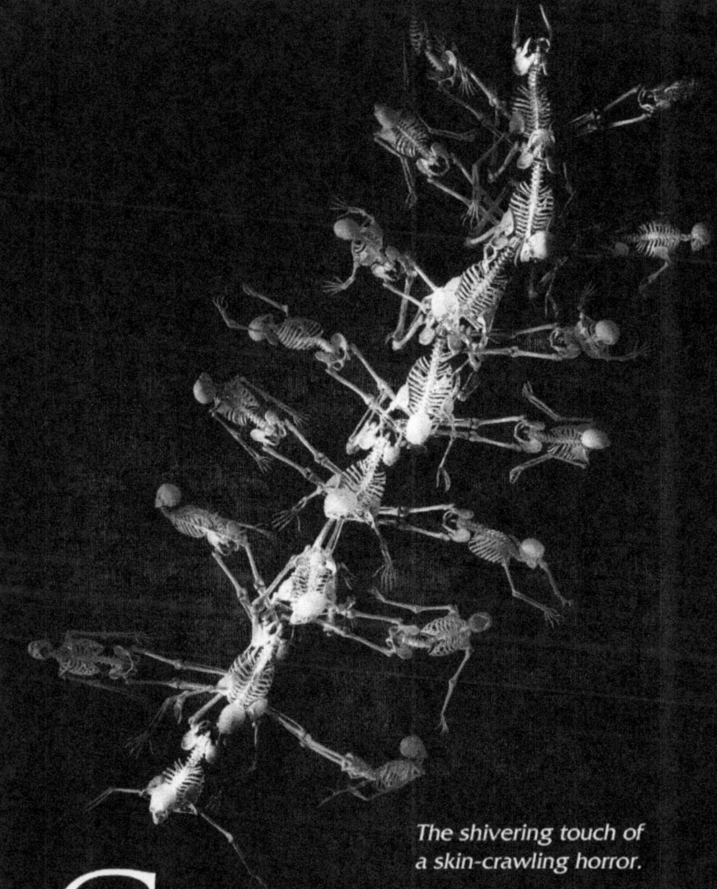
The shivering touch of
a skin-crawling horror.

CHILOPODOPHOBIA

Paul McMahon

Cady entered the house when Uncle Fritch gestured him through the door. Ezzy waited for him at the end of a short hallway. He walked after her, hurrying as she turned right. A doorway to the kitchen stood on the left after he took the turn; he caught a glimpse of an older woman in an apron cooking something that smelled terrific. Ezzy walked past, then took another right. Cady followed and stepped into a large foyer.

He bit his tongue before he could say a word. The wallpaper in here was a dark maroon with an ugly black swirl pattern that swallowed the light. He kept walking, noting the large staircase leading to the second floor and the smallish door beneath it, probably leading to a cellar. He saw a crack in the wall running from the cellar door to the skirt board, and one of the balusters was missing halfway up. The carpet here was dark red and frayed in places along the wall, the woodwork darkly stained. A huge chandelier caught his attention. Only a few candle flame-shaped bulbs shone. Even if every one of the dozens of light bulbs was lit, Cady thought it would still be gloomy in here.

Ezzy turned left through a doorway. Cady glanced

behind him for Uncle Fritch, but he must have gone into the kitchen. He recognized the inside of the front door, mostly because the stone turret stood beside it. The decorative hinges weren't present on this side. A small, arched opening in the turret revealed the start of the spiral staircase Ezzy had told him about.

He walked after her and entered an average-looking study, dark wood and deep red leathers, maroon curtains and brass fittings. A small home bar stood on the left side of the room, but books were lined up on top, where there should be bottles. On the right, the twin windows he'd seen from outside. In front of them sat a worn green couch, its color out of place, angled away from the window and out into the room. Behind it, a tall reading lamp spotlighted the end of the couch. A medical journal was tented on a pillow. Uncle Fritch must have been reading when they'd pulled in.

"This is it," Ezzy said, turning around and leaning against the huge fireplace on the far wall. "Home sweet home."

"Impressive inside and out," Cady said.

"I thought you'd like it."

He took a step toward her, wanting to embrace her just once more before they slipped under Uncle Fritch's more prudish rule, but before he got close, the man cleared his throat from the doorway behind him.

"Ezzy," Fritch said. "Grace is getting dinner ready. Would you be so kind?"

"Of course, Uncle."

Ezzy brushed Cady's shoulder as she headed back

the way they'd come. He watched her go, then spotted Fritch watching him, probably convinced he was staring at her ass. He forced a smile for the old man.

"This'll give us a little time to talk man-to-man," Uncle Fritch said. He glanced into the foyer, then scurried to the bar and reached underneath it. Before Cady could announce that he didn't drink, Uncle Fritch lifted a clear pitcher filled with something pink to the bar.

"Ezzy told me you don't drink," he said. "So I mixed this old family recipe up just for you. It's iced tea sweetened with watermelon. Sounds like a kid's drink, I know, but I guarantee you've never had anything like it."

"Sure, I'll try it," he said. Uncle Fritch dumped ice in a highball glass and then filled it with pink. He pushed Cady's drink across the bar, then dumped two ice cubes into another rocks glass and turned to the bookshelf behind him. "Ezzy's a militant teetotaler," he said. He slid a thick volume of poetry aside and pulled out a bottle of Dewar's Scratched Cask Scotch Whiskey. He splashed two fingers into the glass, downed it, and then poured one finger in its place.

Cady closed his mouth and swallowed.

Fritch tucked the bottle away and replaced the book in front of it. "Between you and me, okay?"

Cady nodded and saluted with his glass of watermelon tea. He rested on the arm of the green sofa. The way it was angled made him want to shove it back against the wall. A quick glance revealed substantial water damage to the window behind it. What he could see of the wall was badly discolored, too.

Fritch settled into the large leather rocking chair across the coffee table from him. He took a deep swallow of his Scotch Whiskey, shut his eyes for a few seconds, and sighed.

Cady sulked at his glass of pink tea.

"Ezzy's told me not to lead with subjects that get my dander up," he said. "Doesn't leave us much to talk about, so I guess it's up to you."

He leveled his gaze directly at Cady and waited. Cady took a slow breath and sipped his drink. The sweetness hit him hard, cloying in its intensity. He swallowed and managed to keep most of the reaction off his face. "This is pretty good, once you get past the sweet," he said.

"It was Ezzy's favorite growing up."

Cady swirled his drink, surprised there were no bits of fruit in it. He took another sip, and this time, prepared for the onslaught, he liked it even more.

"So what do you do with yourself, Cady," Uncle Fritch asked.

"Between jobs, currently, the economy trashed as it is."

Fritch smiled. "The state of the economy is one of those things Ezzy won't let me talk about." The man took a slow swig, as if to rinse away his opinions, then returned his attention to Cady. "What would you be doing if the economy hadn't left you jobless?"

"Retail work, I suppose. Salesman-type stuff. Not that I'm very good at it."

Fritch creased his brow. "If you're not good at it,

why would you choose it?"

"It's easy to do, and it brings in enough money to get by so I can concentrate on my real work, which is playwriting."

Fritch's eyebrows went up. "Playwriting? Unusual. Most people would just say 'writing' and leave it at that."

Cady nodded. "I've done that in the past, but the word encompasses so much it's always followed by the question 'What kind of writing?' which drags a conversation out."

"You don't like long conversations?"

Cady shrugged. "A playwright will live or die by the strength of his dialogue. How could I convince you I was any good if my answer prompted a usual or predictable response?"

Fritch thought for a moment. "What am I going to say next?"

"You're going to ask me if I've written anything you've heard of."

"Exactly what I was thinking."

"I've haven't had anything produced, yet, no."

"Interesting phrasing," Fritch said.

Cady took another sip of his drink. If he wasn't careful, Fritch could start asking about his past, which would not do at all.

"Are you close to your family? Do they live around here?"

"Not especially. I betrayed their expectation that I follow in the family business."

"What business?"

Cady swallowed. Was it his imagination, or was something squiggling beneath Uncle Fritch's collar?

"Furniture," Cady said. "Unfinished."

Fritch downed the last of his drink and stood. He wandered behind the bar again, pausing to run a finger along the spine of the poetry book, and then dumped his ice into the sink with a *clunk*. He reached under the bar and stood with a can of diet soda.

"You shunned your family's retail business so you could work in other people's retail shops?"

"Thus, the nature of their annoyance with me."

Cady downed his own drink and stepped toward the bar. Kid's drink or not, he'd acclimated quickly. His mouth watered while Fritch refilled his glass. When he took it back, it was all he could do not to gulp it down like a man wandering out of the desert.

"Ah, Grace," Fritch said.

Cady turned to see the older woman from the kitchen standing in the doorway. She wrung her hands together just beneath her breasts. Her skin was so pale her hands almost disappeared in front of her white apron.

"Pardon, sir," she said. "Dinner is served."

"Beautiful," Uncle Fritch said. He poured his soda into a glass, then gestured to Cady's drink. "Refill?"

Cady gaped at the empty glass in his hand. It had just been full. When had he done that? In a daze, he handed the glass to Uncle Fritch. His gaze locked onto the edge of the big man's collar. He could have sworn something moved under there.

"I killed my parents when I was thirteen years old."

And now, with the murder of Missy Blake twenty-two years later, it's time for Jack Greene to finish what he started.

When the co-ed's mutilated body is found, the police are clueless, but Jack knows what killed the pretty college student; he's been hunting it for years. The hunt has been going on for too long, though, and Jack wants to end it, but he can't do it alone. The local police aren't equipped to handle the monster in their midst, so Jack recruits Major Kelly Langston, and together they set out to rid the world of this murdering creature once and for all.

A lost child.

A marriage shattered beyond repair?

John Baxter doesn't think so, which is why he has planned this weekend getaway with his wife. He expected a lot of shouting, a lot of tears, but in the end, he hoped to have a stronger foundation upon which they could start rebuilding what they had once had. What he wasn't expecting was the home invasion…and the hell that awaited them beneath the rented cabin.